Prodigal
Gunfighter

Prodigal Gunfighter

Lewis B. Patten

Thorndike Press • Thorndike, Maine

Library of Congress Cataloging in Publication Data

Patten, Lewis B.
  Prodigal gunfighter.

  1. Large type books. I. Title.
[PS3566.A79P7 1982]   813'.54   82-19116
ISBN 0-89621-407-9

Large Print edition available through arrangement with The
New American Library, Inc.

Cover design by Andy Winther.

Prodigal Gunfighter

Chapter 1

At six, Johnny Yoder opened the door of the sheriff's office and stepped out onto the boardwalk. The town of Cottonwood Springs was already stirring under a bright Kansas sun. Shade from giant cottonwoods lining most of its streets threw a dappled pattern of lawns and walks. The sky was a flawless blue. Beyond the town, brown prairie grass rippled in the breeze, looking like a restless sea whenever a gust or whirlwind touched its yielding surface.

The land was almost flat around Cottonwood Springs. Except for the butte half a dozen miles west of town. And except for the bed of Cottonwood Creek which led away to disappear north of the rocky butte.

Yoder stretched, removed his hat and ran a hand through his short-clipped, yellow hair. Scowling he sat down on one of the benches in front of the sheriff's office but there was no relaxation in him. He was tense and jumpy, and there was a smoldering anger in him that would not go away.

He tilted his hat forward against the sun and fished in his pocket for his Bull Durham sack. He rolled a wheatstraw cigarette with strong brown fingers, the backs of which were covered with yellow hair. He licked it and stuck it into his mouth.

With a sudden, angry gesture, he struck a match and touched it to the end of the cigarette. Today was the day. Today, Slade Teplin was coming home.

Slade was already a legend although he was not yet thirty. His name was as well known as that of Wild Bill Hickok, Bat Masterson, Wes Hardin or William Bonney. He had already killed sixteen men. And today he was coming home.

Johnny got up restlessly. He finished his cigarette and tossed it into the street. From a vacant lot next to the jail a shaggy dog approached him, wagging his tail. But this morning Johnny did not reach down to scratch his head as he usually did. He stared up the main street of the town.

A few people were walking along the street. He saw Slade's father, Barney, unlock

8

the door of the bank and go inside just as he had every weekday morning since Johnny first came to Cottonwood Springs three years before. He saw Ern Powers stumble out of the passageway between the Ace-High Saloon and the Emporia. Ern stood blinking against the brilliance of the morning sun before he turned and shuffled unsteadily toward the jail.

Johnny swung his head and glanced down the street. The yellow-framed railroad depot drowsed in the sun, deserted at this hour of the day. Closer, there was Regan's Livery Barn and across from it another, a deserted livery barn that bore across its front the painted legend, "Livery. Est. 1859". Its roofline sagged in the middle, making it look like a swaybacked horse.

Ern Powers reached him. His beard was two days old and his eyes were bloodshot. He looked at Johnny, his glance managing to be both guilty and speculating, then ducked inside. Johnny heard him banging cell doors in the rear as he got the broom and began to sweep.

Johnny turned and walked up the street in the direction of the towering Antlers Hotel. Ern Powers wasn't the only one watching him to see how he was taking the news of

9

Slade Teplin's return. His scowl deepened briefly. What the hell did they expect?

He passed the bank, resisting the impulse to look inside. Barney Teplin probably wasn't looking forward to his son's return any more than Johnny was. Barney had a job as teller in the bank. And John Mc-Cracken, the bank president, was almost fanatical on the subject of public confidence.

He went on, somehow not comforted by the knowledge that his own would not be the only life thrown into turmoil by Slade Teplin's return.

He climbed the two steps to the hotel veranda. This early there were none of the loafers on the porch that usually were here. He went into the vast, cool lobby and crossed the white tile floor to the dining room.

The place was deserted except for Sarah Regan, dressed in a fresh, starched, yellow cotton dress. She wore a checked apron, also yellow, and her dark hair shone warmly in the sun coming through the big front window. She smiled and came toward him.

Johnny managed a thin answering smile. "Coffee ready yet?"

She nodded, her eyes resting steadily on his face. Her smile slowly faded and an anger, almost mirroring his own, suddenly appeared in her eyes. She turned and hurried away, returning a few moments later with a cup and saucer which she put in front of him. She hesitated a moment, then sat down determinedly across from him. She studied his face, her anger fading and being replaced by a kind of exasperated sympathy. She asked, "Why's he coming back after all these years? Why?"

"A lot of people are wondering that."

"Is he going to stay? Or is it just a visit?"

He shrugged, not looking at her now but staring steadily at his cup.

"You think it's her, don't you? You think he's coming back for her."

Johnny was silent for a long, long time. His hands, lying on the table top, gripped each other until the knuckles turned white. At last he said in a tight, thin voice, "She's still his wife."

Sarah nodded, her face suddenly drained of color. "That's what you've got to admit to yourself, Johnny Yoder. That she is his wife. She's not yours and she never will be yours."

He glanced up, his eyes steady and cold. "I came in here for coffee, not advice."

"I don't care what you came in here for. It's the truth."

Johnny gulped the rest of his coffee and stood up. Sarah stood up too. There was a faint shine of tears in her eyes as she said, "I'm sorry, Johnny. I didn't mean . . ."

He nodded. "Sure." He dropped a coin onto the table and headed toward the door. He did not look back and so did not see the tears spilling across Sarah's cheeks.

On the hotel veranda he stopped and tried to roll another cigarette. His fingers shook so badly that he spilled tobacco on the steps in a thin brown stream. He gave up and angrily flung the unfinished cigarette away.

Johnny had never seen Slade Teplin. Neither had he ever hated a man before. But he suddenly admitted to himself that he hated Slade. He hated him enough to want him dead. If Slade was dead, then Molly would be free.

He fished his watch from his pocket and looked at it. It was six-thirty now. Slade's train would not arrive until a little after nine.

He stepped off the hotel veranda and strode down the street toward Regan's Livery. Reaching it, he went inside.

Phil Regan was feeding the horses in the stalls. He stopped what he was doing and stood studying Johnny's face. Johnny said,

"Get my horse for me, Phil."

"Sure, Johnny." Phil shuffled down the long alleyway toward the open rear doors and the sun-washed corral out back.

Johnny watched him go, wondering how a man like Phil Regan could bring forth a daughter like Sarah. Regan returned, shuffling as he always did, leading Johnny's horse.

Johnny flung the blanket and saddle on while Regan watched. He cinched the saddle down, feeling Regan's steady glance. As he put a foot into the stirrup, Regan said, "They say he's fast, Johnny, faster'n any man alive."

Johnny grunted noncommittally as he hit the saddle.

Regan asked, "Reckon anybody'll try an' take him while he's here?" There was an eager light in his eyes. He licked his lips as though imagining such a fight.

Johnny said sourly, "You'd like it if somebody did, wouldn't you? Even if it cost that man his life?"

Regan grinned crookedly. "Why don't you try him, Johnny? You'd come closer'n anybody in town. An' you got reason to want him dead."

Johnny touched spurs to his horse's sides.

13

The startled animal leaped toward the door and thundered through. Johnny reined him aside and pounded down the street and across the railroad tracks.

His eyes glazed. His mouth was a thin, hard line. He supposed everyone in town was silently thinking what Regan had just said to him. They all knew he had been seeing Molly for almost a year. They knew he wanted to marry her. They also knew she was still Slade Teplin's wife.

There were even those who said Slade was coming home because of Johnny Yoder's attentions to his wife. They said Slade was coming home to kill again.

Johnny raked his horse savagely with the spurs. He thundered along the road that bordered Cottonwood Creek as it wound aimlessly toward the butte.

For a moment he almost hoped Slade was coming home to kill him, even though he knew it wasn't true. Slade had left his wife five years before. He hadn't returned to see her once. He probably didn't even care.

A mile from town there was a small frame house just at the edge of the cottonwoods bordering the creek. There was a tiny patch of lawn in front, a garden in back. Both lawn and garden were watered patiently with pails Molly carried from the creek. Johnny dismounted and tied his horse to the limb of a scrubby cottonwood. He walked toward the door.

Molly taught school in town. But she never left here until seven and it was not yet that late. Johnny knocked and waited impatiently.

The door opened. And suddenly all the anger, all the irritation was gone from Johnny, driven away as dew is driven away by the morning sun.

She stood aside to let him enter, but her welcoming smile was weak and forced. She seemed excessively pale to him. Her eyes revealed the fact that if she had slept at all last night it had been a short and uneasy sleep.

He crossed the kitchen to the table and sat down. Molly Teplin asked, "Are you hungry, Johnny? I can fix something for you in a minute."

He shook his head. "Just coffee, thanks."

He watched her as she got cup and saucer from the cupboard, then crossed to the stove to fill the cup. Her back was slim and straight. Her hair, worn in a demure bun at the nape of her neck, was a burnished copper color that shone almost like metal in the early morning sunlight streaming through the open door.

Her skin was white and there was a bridge of tiny freckles across her nose. Her eyes were sometimes green and sometimes blue, depending upon the light. There was a sudden ache in his chest and he wondered how Slade, or any man, could leave her.

She gave him his coffee and sat down across from him. She picked up her fork and tried to eat but after the first mouthful she gave up. "I can't eat, Johnny. I can't sleep. I can't even think. Why is he coming back now? Why, after almost five years?"

He shook his head miserably. "The important thing is not that he's coming back, but what you're going to do about it. Are you going to let him come back to you?"

He wouldn't look at her as he asked the question, but stared instead at his coffee cup.

She murmured, "I don't know. Oh, Johnny, I don't know!"

He looked up and met her glance steadily with his own. He said, "Molly, I love you. I want to marry you. He deserted you five years ago. A week ago you were going to get a divorce from him and marry me. But since you heard he was coming back . . ."

16

He watched her, noting the way her glance dropped away from his. He felt a flash of sudden anger, thinking for a fleeting instant that her love for him was too thin and weak a thing to remain steadfast now.

Then, as suddenly as his anger had come, it was gone again. He knew why Molly was considering letting Slade Teplin come back to her. She thought Slade knew Johnny was courting her. She believed Slade had heard she intended divorcing him. She thought Slade was coming back to kill Johnny, and she was willing to become Slade's wife again to save his life.

He got up and went around the table to her. He stood looking down, watching the flush that crept into her neck and face. He said, "Molly, stand up."

She stood up reluctantly, but she would not look up at his face.

Very gently, he put out his hands. He took her shoulders and drew her close. He could feel her body trembling. He could feel, suddenly, his own wild hunger blazing up . . .

His arms tightened savagely, crushing her against his chest. He said in a choking voice, "No! You're not to go back to him! If you do . . . I'll kill him, Molly. I swear to God I will!"

She looked up, tears welling from her eyes and spilling across her cheeks. Her voice was a tortured cry, "Johnny, what am I going to do! What am I going to do?"

"Tell him he can't come back to you. Tell him you're going to marry me."

"He'll – He might – Johnny, you wouldn't have a chance against Slade."

"Let me worry about that. You just let me worry about that."

She drew away. "I've got to go to school. The children . . ."

"Looks like you'd have called off school for today." He tried to make his voice as normal as he could.

"Because Slade is coming home? I can't think of a worse reason for a holiday. They're making a hero out of him as it is."

She began to gather up the dishes. Johnny said, "I'll hitch up your buggy horse."

He went out, crossed the yard to the small stable at the rear of the house and went inside. He harnessed her old, swaybacked buggy horse, led him out and backed him between the buggy shafts. By the time he was finished, Molly was ready, holding several books and a sack lunch in her hands.

Johnny took them from her and put them into the buggy. He helped her up. He got his own horse and led him to the buggy, intending to tie him behind, but Molly stopped him. "No, Johnny. Not this morning. Let me drive in alone today. Enough tongues are wagging as it is."

He stared at her, hurt and obscurely angry at himself because he was. She made a faint smile that failed to hide the lingering pain in her eyes. She slapped the horse's back with the reins and the horse trotted away toward town.

Johnny stood looking after her for a long, long time. Then he mounted and slowly followed her, a quarter mile behind.

Chapter 2

It was almost seven when Johnny Yoder reached town. He rode up the street to the jail, swung down and tied his horse to the rail out front. Molly's buggy was out of sight, having turned off Main Street at the upper end of town.

He went inside. Ern Powers had finished with the cells and there was an odor of disinfectant in the air. Ern was sweeping the office as Johnny came in. He glanced up.

Johnny grinned humorlessly at him. "Big night last night?"

Ern nodded guiltily. He leaned on the broom, stared at the floor a moment, then glanced up at Johnny again. "I don't know why I do it. I never intend to when I start. I just don't know when to quit."

Johnny sat down at the sheriff's roll-top desk. He stretched his long legs out in front of him.

He heard steps on the boardwalk outside and glanced up. Arch Schilling came in, leaving the door standing open behind him. He looked at Johnny, then at Ern, then crossed the room and hung his hat on the coat tree.

He glanced back at Johnny and said what he'd said each morning for the past three years. "Had breakfast yet?"

"I'll go get some now."

Johnny got to his feet, waited a moment expectantly to see if the sheriff would bring up the subject of Slade Teplin's return. When Arch said nothing, Johnny glanced at him.

He surprised Arch studying him speculatively and grinned. Arch grinned back but did not speak. For an instant there was a closeness between them, an understanding that did not need words.

Arch was a big, rawboned man, sixty on his last birthday. His face was like the map of Kansas, brown and weathered and deeply furrowed by the erosion of the years. His eyes were the blue of a Kansas sky, surrounded by tiny crowfoot wrinkles that deepened when he smiled. His mouth was a slash, hard and tough and uncompromising above a chin equally uncompromising and tough. He had been a cattleman until he was elected sheriff five years ago. He didn't know all there was to know about law enforcement, maybe, but he knew Kansas like he knew the back of his hand. He could trail like an Indian and he wasn't afraid of anything.

Arch said now, gruffly, "Go on and eat. You want to meet the train, don't you?"

Johnny grinned again and went out into the brilliant sun. He hesitated a moment between the hotel dining room and Ho's Restaurant, not wanting to listen to another lecture from Sarah, but in the end he chose the hotel. He'd just as well eat where he usually did. If he didn't, people would say he was trying to hide.

He walked up the street toward the hotel. There were more people on the walks now. Some of them nodded or spoke to Johnny and he returned their greetings as normally as he could. He could feel them all watching him, and occasionally he would catch that speculating look in someone's eyes.

He wondered if there would be any pressure on Arch to put Slade on as a deputy. Cottonwood Springs was a flyspeck on the Kansas map. Half the people in Kansas didn't even know that it existed. It hadn't been too prosperous since the trail drives stopped coming up from Texas several years before. It was a town that was slowly dying on the vine.

Slade Teplin could change all that. If he was a sheriff's deputy he would give Cottonwood Springs a kind of fame. People would come here just to see him.

Some of the merchants wouldn't want prosperity if its price was bullets in the streets. But there were probably others who wouldn't care.

He reached the hotel. There were half a dozen loafers on the veranda now. One called, "Going to meet the train, Johnny?"

He glanced at the man and nodded. He forced himself to grin. "Everybody else will be meeting it so I guess I'd just as well." His words brought an uneasy laugh from the group on the sunny porch.

He went into the hotel and across the lobby to the dining room. He sat down at his accustomed table next to one of the windows from which he could look into the street.

Mostly, the sheriff's job in Cottonwood County was a tame one nowadays. Arch Schilling and Johnny Yoder served papers. They jailed a few drunks on Saturday night.

They mediated a midnight quarrel between a husband and wife. They caught a kid who had broken a store window with a rock.

These were the everyday things. Occasionally they were called upon to handle something more serious. But Johnny could number the serious crimes that had occurred here in the past three years on the fingers of one hand.

The peaceful quality of Cottonwood Springs would change with Slade Teplin's arrival home. He would draw men from everywhere. Just his presence here would accomplish that. They'd come to look at him and talk to him. Or they'd come to try him out — to see if he was really as good as he was supposed to be. Whoever managed to kill Slade Teplin would thereby gain instant fame for himself. And there were plenty of men who wanted that kind of fame.

Sarah Regan came and stood beside his table. There was no longer anger in her face. It was pale and drawn. She said, "I'm sorry, Johnny. I had no right to say the things I said to you a while ago."

He didn't feel like smiling but he did. He reached out, took her hand and squeezed it lightly. "Forget it, Sarah. I'm sorry too."

Her face flushed with pleasure and he

released her hand. He said, "I'll have a steak. And some eggs."

Sarah turned hurriedly and walked away toward the kitchen. Johnny let his glance wander over those in the dining room. Most of the people looked away, avoiding his glance. Others nodded or spoke to him almost with embarrassment.

They knew about Molly. Half of them or more probably figured there would be a gunfight down at the railroad station the minute Slade Teplin stepped off the train.

Johnny turned his head and stared out the window. What if they were right? What if Slade had heard about him and Molly and was coming back to kill?

He was surprised when Sarah set his breakfast in front of him. He hadn't realized that so much time had passed. He pulled out his watch and glanced at it. It was almost eight o'clock.

Sarah hurried away, flustered and embarrassed now. Johnny watched her go, wondering why he'd had to fall in love with a married woman instead of with Sarah. He scowled at his food, eating doggedly, forcing himself even though he didn't feel like eating anything. All he had to do was leave his food untouched and within half an hour

25

everybody in town would be saying he was scared half out of his wits.

He grinned wryly to himself. If he had any sense, maybe he would be scared. He didn't know Slade Teplin, except by reputation. He had no idea how deep Slade Teplin's pride was. The man might even care for his wife in spite of the five years he had been away from her.

He finished his breakfast and laid a quarter beside his plate. He rolled a cigarette, surprised that his fingers were steady now. He lighted it and rose.

He walked out, crammed on his hat and stepped onto the veranda. He glanced up and down the street, then headed for the jail.

Another hour, he thought. Another hour to wait.

Damn Teplin anyway! He had the whole town in a state of nerves. He had accomplished that simply by telegraphing his father that he was coming home.

Arch Schilling was sittong on one of the benches in front of the jail when he reached the place. He was staring downstreet at the railroad depot, at the people already beginning to gather there. Johnny sat down beside him. "What's he like?" he asked.

"Slade? I don't know what he's like now. But I remember him as a boy." Arch's forehead creased into a light frown. He was silent for several moments, then he said, "His mother died when he was twelve – same age as Tommy, my grandson. Barney went to pieces when she died. He didn't come out of the house for damn near two weeks. I guess he hardly ate. Slade stayed with the neighbors and with the Newcombs over at the parsonage. Barney began to drink."

He was silent long enough to pack his pipe and light it. "Barney got pretty bad. He lost the house or sold it or something. I don't know. He used to sleep in that old livery barn across from Regan's place. Or he'd sleep wherever it was that he passed out."

"What about Slade? What did he do?"

"He worked for his keep, one place or another. He was a sour-faced, sullen kid. He did his work but it was like he hated the town and everyone in it. I used to come in to town once a week in those days for supplies. He was working at Zachary's Mercantile at the time. He'd help me load up and I tried a time or two to be nice to him. He'd just look at me and then turn and

27

walk away. Like he hated me too and, hell, he didn't hardly know me."

Johnny rolled a cigarette and lighted it. There was a sizable crowd, now, down at the railroad station. Most of them were just standing around, but a few of the men had gathered into a group and were talking heatedly. Johnny said, "If he hated the town I wonder why he's coming back."

"He might be coming back for you, Johnny. Have you thought of that?"

"Yeah. I've thought of it, but I don't believe it. He hasn't seen her for five years. Why the hell should he care?"

"Pride. He doesn't want her, but he's damned if anyone else is going to have her either. Not in front of everybody in this town anyway."

Johnny didn't speak. He shrugged, and at last he said, "Well, if he feels that way, I guess I'll be number seventeen on his list. Unless I just happen to be lucky today."

"Leave your gun here when you go down to the station."

"What good would that do? I can't leave it off forever."

Arch pulled thoughtfully on his pipe. After a while Johnny asked, "How'd he get started — with his gun I mean?"

"I think he was about eighteen or nineteen. He'd been packing a gun for a couple of years, practicing with it all the time. I think that gun was his way of showing the town that he was someone. Anyway, some drifter began funnin' him about it. First thing you know, Slade yanked it out. He gave that drifter the damndest cussin' I ever heard." Arch shrugged lightly. "It ended like you'd expect. The drifter yanked his own gun out and ended up dead in the street right in front of the Emporia."

"Was that when Slade went away?"

"No. There was a trial. The jury acquitted him in spite of the fact that he drew first. I guess they figured the drifter started it. And I guess they felt sorry for Slade. Barney never took a drink afterward, though. He straightened up and rented a house for the two of them, but I guess it was just too late. Slade left town a few months later and didn't come back until about six years ago. He married Molly and they stayed here for a while. Nobody would give Slade a job, and finally he took her away. She came back alone and she's been here ever since."

Johnny looked at his watch. It was almost nine o'clock. He stood up and surprised himself by nervously straightening his gun belt. He grinned self-consciously at Arch.

Arch said, "Leave it here. You don't know . . ."

Johnny shook his head stubbornly. "If I leave my gun here I'll be letting him know – well hell, more than just that I'm afraid of him. I'll be telling him that I'm ashamed – of what's between Molly and me. I'll be telling the whole town the same thing. And I'm not ashamed. Not one damn bit."

"All right, Johnny. Have it your own way." Arch's voice plainly said that he disapproved, but there was something else in it as well, something that was not disapproval at all.

Distantly, Johnny heard the mournful whistle of the train. He said, "Here it comes."

Arch Schilling got ponderously to his feet. "Let's go."

Side by side they paced down the walk toward the railroad station. Johnny grinned to himself. Everyone waiting on the station platform was turned their way, watching them.

Johnny heard steps on the boardwalk behind him and turned his head. Barney Teplin was walking along about a quarter block behind. His face was white and strained and he looked fifteen years older than he had looked yesterday.

Johnny suddenly felt sorry for him. He knew how he'd feel if he lost Molly — as if nothing in the world mattered anymore. He could understand how Barney had felt when he lost his wife.

But Barney had lost a lot more than his wife. He had lost his son as well. And now the ghost of what had once been his son was coming back — to taunt him before the whole town of Cottonwood Springs.

Johnny didn't believe that Slade was after him. But he was sure of one thing. Before Slade left town he would kill again.

Chapter 3

Johnny Yoder could see the train as soon as he stepped onto the station platform. It was about half a mile away, pouring smoke from its stack, coming on fast.

He felt his irritability rise because no one was watching the train. Everybody on the station platform was watching him.

He turned his head and glanced uptown, thinking of Molly and knowing how she would be feeling as she listened to the train's long, mournful whistle. She probably had her hands full keeping order in the school. The kids must be even more excited over Slade's coming than their parents were.

The engine slowed for the station, then came puffing past the platform to stop just beyond it. There were two coaches and a caboose.

Johnny resisted the impulse to loosen his gun in its holster. His palms felt clammy and he wiped them surreptitiously on the sides of his pants legs. He felt his anger rise, but now it was anger at himself. He wasn't afraid of Slade. In spite of Slade's reputation, he wasn't afraid to face the man. Then why this nervousness?

It had nothing to do with physical fear, he realized. But it was fear just the same. Fear that Slade Teplin would take Molly away from him. Fear that Slade would force her to come back to him by threatening Johnny's life.

A man got off the first coach, a fat man carrying a valise. A woman followed, then turned and helped her two children down the steps. A man followed her children, a gray-haired man almost as old as Arch, dressed in range clothes so rumpled it looked as though he had slept in them for a week.

Johnny switched his glance to the second coach. A young woman got off, a pretty woman whose clothes told Johnny instantly that she was a saloon girl. An elderly Mexican woman followed her. And behind the older Mexican woman came a man who had to be Slade.

He was not a big man. He was not as tall as Johnny, nor was he as broad. He was dressed in a black suit, the coat of which was unbuttoned to allow free access to the holstered gun which sagged low against his right side. He wore a narrow-brimmed black hat.

Two things caught and held Johnny's attention instantly. One was the way Slade Teplin moved, with an almost feline grace. His feet came down softly, almost stealthily as he walked, and Johnny got the feeling that no matter what he did, or how he moved, he would never be off balance for a single instant.

The second thing that held Johnny's attention was his face. His eyes seemed almost black. And they came as close to being expressionless as any pair of eyes Johnny had ever seen.

Studying the man's face, he realized that not only the eyes created the impression of expressionlessness. The whole face contributed.

Teplin paused half a dozen steps from the coach. He carried a small valise in his left hand. His glance swept over the crowd, which was frozen and silent, and came to rest on Johnny. He held Johnny's eyes for a moment, then looked briefly at the star on Johnny's shirt. His glance fell away and touched Arch Schilling before it went on to

Barney Teplin, standing just beyond Johnny and the sheriff.

Ignoring the crowd, he walked toward Barney. Johnny felt his muscles tense as Slade approached. He saw, out of the corner of his eye, the way the crowd faded away behind Slade. He could hear them moving away from behind him, and his mouth twisted almost imperceptibly. They were getting out of the line of fire. They still thought Slade might shoot it out with Johnny, right here and now.

Johnny knew Slade was aware of him as the man went past. He could feel it, sense it. He also knew Slade would do nothing now.

Slade stopped immediately in front of his father. Johnny turned to watch. He could not see Slade's face, but he could see Barney's. It was almost gray and it shone with perspiration. It mirrored so many conflicting emotions that it would have been bard for Johnny to say which of them was strongest, uppermost.

There was anger in Barney Teplin's face. There was a kind of forlorn joy at seeing his son again. There was shame, because of what his son was, what he had become, and because he knew a large part of blame for it lay with him. And there was puzzlement, because he could not guess why his son had now come back.

Slade looked beyond his father's face at the town. His voice was flat, almost as expressionless as his face. "It looks the same. It hasn't changed a bit."

"No." Barney seemed to have no words. The two stood facing each other in awkward silence for a long, long time. At last Barney said, "Come on. I've got the morning off."

He turned and Slade paced beside him, across the street and up Main on the shady side of the street. The crowd made a low murmur of disappointment that increased in volume as men began talking to each other in low, almost resentful tones. Johnny turned his head and grinned at Arch. "He disappointed 'em. They thought there was going to be some excitement."

Arch muttered, "The hell with 'em." He walked to the end of the station platform and stepped off into the dusty street. Johnny kept pace with him.

Halfway to the jail Arch asked, "What do you think of him?"

Johnny didn't reply. He was still trying to sort his impressions within his own thoughts. Slade Teplin knew about Molly and him. That impression had been very plain and clear. Yet he had sensed no particular anger in the man over it.

It followed, therefore, that the town had been wrong. Slade's pride had not brought him to Cottonwood Springs to kill.

Then what had brought him back? Assuming this was not simply a brief visit, what was here strong enough to draw Slade Teplin back?

Only one answer to that. Molly. She had to be the reason for Slade's return.

An even more sinister bit of reasoning followed. Slade would use Johnny to get her back. Knowing she might well refuse after five years, he would threaten to kill Johnny unless she did come back to him.

Johnny cursed softly under his breath. Arch said, "Yeah. I saw the way he looked at you. He knows about you and Molly, but he didn't come back to get rid of you or he'd have done it on the station platform a few minutes ago. He came back for Molly and he'll use you to get her to come back to him."

"Or else he just plain doesn't give a damn."

Arch nodded.

Johnny asked, "What's he going to do for

a living, Arch? Maybe he's got a little money, but it won't last forever. He'll have to do something and he sure as hell won't be getting a job through Barney at the bank."

"No. John McCracken wouldn't have him around. There's only one thing he's fitted for, Johnny, and you know what it is as well as me."

"Law enforcement, huh?"

"Yep. And since I'm elected, that just leaves your job. You're in his way in more ways than one."

Johnny was silent until they reached the jail. Then he turned his head and looked at Arch. "You're the sheriff. You do the hiring and firing of your deputies. You going to give my job to him?"

Arch grinned. "No sir. You don't need to worry about that."

Arch went into the office, but Johnny stayed out on the walk in front. Slade Teplin and his father had disappeared, having turned the corner and headed for Barney's house. The crowd that had been at the railroad station was dispersing, streaming up the street past the jail, headed for the two saloons. The girl who had been on the train was carrying her valise in the same direction.

She stopped when she reached Johnny. She looked at the star on his shirt and smiled in a way that was both placating and defiant. She asked, "How many saloons in town? Just those two?"

Johnny nodded. She was pretty, he saw, and perhaps a year or two younger than he. But there was a quality in her that was older than her years. She asked, "You got laws in this town against a girl working in a saloon?"

Johnny shok his head. He said, "Try the Emporia."

"Thanks, I will." She seemed relieved. She hesitated a moment more, as though trying to think of something light to say. Then she gave up, shrugged wearily, and went on up the street.

Cal Reeder stopped, not looking at Johnny but at the girl's hips as she walked. "Nice, huh?"

Johnny nodded. He studied Cal neutrally. He didn't really dislike Cal, but he couldn't say he liked him either. Cal wore a gun much the way Slade Teplin wore his, low against his side in an open holster. The grips were smooth and shiny with use. Cal fancied himself a gunman, but he'd never drawn his gun against a man and he probably never would.

He was a tall young man, about twenty-three, Johnny guessed. His hair was black. His jaws showed a faint shadow of black stubble. His eyes were brown, his face narrow. His father had a ranch not far from Arch Schilling's ranch, but Cal stayed in town most of the time. He only went home when he went broke.

Cal watched the girl, his eyes bright, until she disappeared into the Emporia. Then he turned his head and looked at Johnny's face. "What did you think of him?"

"Slade? I don't know. I guess I haven't decided what I think of him."

"You think he's as fast as they say?"

"You don't kill sixteen men by being slow."

"Yeah, but maybe none of them was fast — really fast I mean."

Johnny looked at him wearily. He knew what Cal was leading up to. He also knew Cal wouldn't be the only young buck in Cottonwood County with the same idea. He said, "Forget it. He could put a hole in you before you got the hammer back."

"Maybe. Maybe not. I'm pretty good." Cal pivoted suddenly to face the railroad station. He crouched slightly as he turned and his hand shot to the grip of his gun. He brought it out, leveled it, but he did not thumb the hammer back. He holstered the gun and looked at Johnny's face.

Johnny shook his head again. "Forget it, Cal. Even if you beat him, which you wouldn't, what would it get you in the end? You know how a man like Slade lives? He goes from town to town and in every one he's invited to move on. Every place he goes, there's someone who wants to try him out. Most of the sixteen he's killed were men like that. Young bucks like you who figure he made his reputation by killing cripples and old men."

"I didn't say that."

Johnny grinned at him. "You as much as said it. You said maybe none of the sixteen was really fast."

"You talk like a damned old man yourself." There was resentment in Cal's eyes. "Maybe you'll end up number seventeen. As soon as Slade finds out you been foolin' around with his wife."

Johnny's voice was suddenly like a whip. "Doing what?"

A dull flush crept into Cal's narrow face. "You know what I mean. Seeing her. Goin' with her. What are you so damned ringy about?"

41

Johnny didn't reply. He was still angry, but he was also aware Cal had meant no slur. He said, "All right. All right."

Cal walked on up the street, heading toward the Emporia. Johnny saw him go inside.

He suddenly wanted a drink himself, but he didn't want to go into either of the saloons. He'd had enough for now of the townsmen's speculating looks. Besides, he knew they would be placing bets in both saloons. Even money Slade would call on Johnny before a week was out. Two to one, probably, that he'd kill Johnny when he did.

Filled with sour anger, he went into the office. How long was he supposed to wait for Slade to make up his mind what he was going to do? How long?

Arch was thumbing through wanted posters. He had an inch thick pile of them on his desk. He looked up. "He ain't in here."

"You didn't think he would be, did you?"

"Nope. Just thought I'd look."

Johnny began to pace nervously back and forth, like a caged mountain lion. Arch said, "Ease off. The first move is up to him and you know it is."

Johnny stopped pacing and glared at him.

He said fiercely, "I'm sick of him. The son-of-a-bitch hasn't been here an hour and I'm sick of him. Why the hell can't we just tell him to move on — to get out of town? Other towns do and they get away with it."

"This one's different. Because this is his home. Ease off, Johnny. That didn't sound like you at all."

Johnny forced a sour grin. "Maybe not. But I feel so damned helpless! Molly's even considering it — going back with him. She says its because she's his wife, but it isn't that at all. She's afraid I'll fight with him. And she's afraid that if I do, I'll be killed." He paced back and forth a while longer, then whirled and faced the sheriff angrily. "Maybe I'll just hunt him up and order him out of town. Maybe I'll do the forcing for a change."

"He'd kill you, Johnny. You'd just be committing suicide. And he'd still be alive."

"Maybe not. Maybe if I worked it right I could take him along with me."

Arch got out of the swivel chair. He put a hand on Johnny's shoulder. "Go easy, son. Go easy. You don't even know he's going to stay."

Johnny shook off his hand and went to the window. He stared out angrily. The sun

43

still shone brightly in the street. But to Johnny it seemed as though a cloud had drifted across the face of the sun. The town was in shadow since Slade Teplin had come home. And the shadow wouldn't be gone until Slade was gone – or until he was dead.

Chapter 4

It was a relief to Barney Teplin when he and Slade turned off Main Street and he could no longer feel the curious stares of those at the railroad station.

He felt ill-at-ease with Slade, and a couple of times turned his head to look at his son's impassive face. It was cold and impersonal, without visible feeling of any kind.

Barney wondered briefly if Slade knew about Johnny Yoder and Molly. He supposed he did. It was probably the reason for Slade's return. Yet Slade had showed no animosity toward Johnny at the station. He had glanced at him, true, but there had been no expression on his face.

Not that that meant anything, he thought. Slade's face just didn't show expression. It didn't now and it hadn't then.

He asked, "How long are you going to stay?"

Slade didn't reply. Barney looked at him and Slade, feeling his father's regard, shrugged.

Barney began to feel anger stirring in his mind. He asked suddenly, "Why *did* you come back? The way you hate this town, I'd think you'd *want* to stay away."

Slade looked at him mildly. "You forget. This is my home. You're here and so is my wife."

"Wife! You haven't seen her or written her for almost five years. You've only written me once, a couple of weeks ago."

He kept his glance steadily on his son's face, trying to fathom from it what was in Slade's mind, knowing Slade wouldn't tell him in words. He surprised in Slade's eyes, suddenly, a burning flash of hatred so strong it seemed to shrivel him. He said, "You hate me. You hate this town. I think you even hate your wife."

The revealing gleam was gone almost instantly. Slade looked at him indulgently. "You're imagining things. Your conscience bothers you and you imagine things."

Barney felt baffled, ineffectual. A couple of twelve-year-olds, their eyes wide with awe, came from behind a lilac bush and began to follow them. One of them was Tommy Schilling, the sheriff's grandson.

Tommy said shrilly, "It's him all right. He wouldn't be with Mr. Teplin if he wasn't Slade."

The boys stayed a discreet hundred feet behind. Barney smiled wryly to himself, thinking that if Slade turned his head they would probably run like scared rabbits. They must have sneaked away from school during recess.

Slade asked suddenly, "What's she doing these days?"

"Teaching school. Even Slade Teplin's wife has to eat, you know. And God knows you never sent her anything."

Slade stopped suddenly. Barney, a step beyond, stopped too and turned to face his son. Again that burning hatred was in Slade's eyes. And again it seemed to shrivel Barney's soul.

Slade said, "Don't talk to me about obligations, old man. You had one to me after my mother died. But you wanted to hide in a bottle and you didn't give a good goddamn about me. I lived like a stray dog."

Barney opened his mouth to justify himself, then closed it as suddenly as he'd opened it. Words would not undo the damage that had been done. Besides, Barney wasn't so sure there *was* justification for what he'd done.

Yet when he thought back, whenever he thought of Mary . . . the pain still came, so sharp and bitter it was almost unbearable. That pain had driven him to drink. That and the feeling that there was nothing left in the world for him with Mary gone.

Only liquor had been able to dull his pain. Without liquor he would probably have shot himself.

Yet he knew Slade was also right. A boy shouldn't have to grow up alone. He shouldn't have to shift for himself and live like a stray dog in an unfriendly world. Barney said softly, "I'm sorry, Slade. If I could undo the things I did to you . . ."

"I've done all right in spite of it. I'm the town's most famous citizen."

A crawling uneasiness touched Barney's heart. His chest felt tight. For an instant he saw unrelieved evil in Slade.

He shook that feeling off by sheer force of will, studying his son's face, searching desperately for something else.

He found it to his own inexpressible relief. It was a kind of hurt, little boy quality far back in the depths of Slade's dark eyes. It was the look you see in the eyes of a child just before they flood with tears.

Then, as quickly as it had come, it was gone. And Slade was grinning a twisted, sardonic grin. "Come on. Let's get on home. Before those damned kids ask if they can hold my gun."

Barney resumed his steady pacing at his son's side. They reached the small, one-story house Barney occupied, and Barney held the gate for Slade.

The fence was neat, a picket fence painted white. The lawn was beginning to get a little dry, but it was neatly cut. The house had recently been painted. Barney had done the work himself, evenings and Saturday afternoons.

It was the house Barney had rented so many years before, after Slade's first killing jolted him out of his grief. He owned it now, having bought it, over a period of time, out of his earnings at the bank.

Slade asked, as they climbed the two steps to the porch, "You live here alone?"

Barney nodded. He realized suddenly that he had never considered anything else. True, there had been times when he had needed a woman and at times the hunger for one had been almost unbearable. Yet he had always felt so guilty and disloyal because of it that he had never sought one out. And marriage was out of the question for him. He did not even want a housekeeper. Her presence in his house would have seemed like a blasphemy.

Orville Newcomb, the town preacher, had told him many times he ought to get married again. He had told him prolonged grief twisted and warped a man. He had emphasized the fact that Mary was dead and gone and that Barney was still alive, with a life of his own to live. He had tried to convince Barney that Mary would have wanted him to remarry and be content once more.

But Mary still lived in Barney's heart. She would never die, he knew, as long as he kept her there.

He opened the front door and Slade went inside. He looked around the room, his face like carved stone. There were things in this room he remembered from his boyhood, Barney realized. There were some of Mary's things. Slade said suddenly, "I want a drink."

Barney went into the kitchen and got a dusty bottle of whisky from a cupboard. He took it, with a glass, to his son.

Slade said, "Do I have to drink alone? On my first day home?"

Barney said, "I haven't touched it for over

ten years. I don't even want it any more. You go ahead."

Slade said, "Pa . . ."

Barney suddenly felt a burning behind his eyes. He hadn't been much of a father to Slade. Slade had gone a long way, but he was not yet thirty now. A lot of his life lay ahead of him. He could change. He could spend the rest of his life making up for all that had gone before. But if his own father refused to help . . .

Barney said suddenly, "I'll get another glass. We'll drink to your coming home."

He went to the kitchen and took down another glass. He brought it into the parlor and Slade poured it about half full. Slade filled his own glass similarly.

Slade raised it. "To my coming home."

Barney raised his glass. The odor of the whisky was strong, acrid, biting in his nostrils. For some reason, the odor reminded him of waking up on a cold winter morning in the alley behind the Emporia. It reminded him of another smell, the smell of his own body and reeking clothes after a week-long drunk. It reminded him of how hard it had been to think, those days, because liquor had drugged and dulled his mind.

But Slade was watching him, waiting to

drink until his father drank. He put the glass to his lips and suddenly gulped the stuff.

It burned. It gagged him and made him cough. But suddenly he realized how much he had missed that taste, how much he had missed the warm burn of whisky coursing down his throat, lying like a comforting warmth in his stomach afterward.

He held out his glass and Slade re-filled it. Slade was sipping his own drink. He was smiling at Barney and Barney realized this was the first time he had seen Slade really smile. Yet there was a quality about Slade's smile that troubled him. He studied his son's face, trying to isolate that quality in his thoughts.

Slade's face seemed blurry and far away. Barney's head felt light. After more than ten years, he thought, it didn't take much to set a man off. In the old days, half a glass of whisky had been just a starter.

He gulped about half of the whisky in his glass. Again it burned all the way down, and lay like hot coals in his stomach. Again the taste brought back memories.

Through the curtain whisky had lowered across his mind, he peered at his son's face. It was still smiling, but the smile was strained.

And once more he had the vague impression he was looking at something unbelievably evil. He whispered hoarsely, "Why did you come back?"

Slade chuckled softly. Barney blinked, trying to see his son's face more clearly through the thickening haze. He wanted to lie down now and sleep. He lifted the glass to his mouth and finished it.

Anger came to him suddenly, and it was white-hot when it came. He shouted thickly, "Why? Damn you, why did you come back?"

"You'll know soon enough. Here. You'd just as well finish this." Slade extended the bottle.

Barney swung blindly. His hand struck the bottle and knocked it halfway across the room. It didn't break, but he could hear its contents gurgling as they ran out on the rug.

And he knew, suddenly, why Slade had come back. Not for peace. Not for Molly. Not for an end to the challenges that a gunfighter's fame draws to him like iron filings are drawn to a magnet. Not for any of these things. Not for anything good.

Hatred had spawned the speed in Slade Teplin's hand. Hatred had made his gun belch death sixteen different times. And hatred had brought him here. Hatred for Barney, his father. Hatred for the town. Hatred for all mankind.

Death would walk the streets of Cottonwood Springs before Slade Teplin was gone again. Unless he was killed, now, like a rabid dog.

Barney got up unsteadily. He mumbled something about being back. He left the room and went into the bedroom where he slept. Carefully, he got his shotgun from the closet, the one he used sometimes for hunting prairie chickens or quail. He loaded it with fingers that trembled almost uncontrollably. He snapped the action shut.

He turned, hearing the door behind him. He tried desperately to bring the gun to bear.

Slade was too quick for him. He took one swift step and yanked the shotgun out of Barney's hands.

His face was white and terrible. His eyes seemed to Barney as though they glowed like coals. He broke the action of the gun and ejected the two shells Barney had loaded it with.

Deliberately he turned his back on Barney. He returned to the parlor. Barney staggered to the bedroom door.

For an instant he thought Slade had gone completely mad. He held the gun by its double barrel and he swung it like a club. He smashed everything he could, vases, lamps, mirrors, furniture. The gunstock broke but he went on smashing, with just the barrel now.

His eyes blazed crazily. His face was white. Sweat streamed from his face. His breath came in short, exhausted gasps.

The room began to whirl eerily before Barney Teplin's eyes. He felt himself falling, felt the impact of the floor. Then he was unconscious and mercifully knew no more.

Chapter 5

The Cottonwood Springs school sat at the very edge of town, with the endless prairie its backyard.

It was a single-story frame building, containing two rooms and a cloakroom. Out back there were two outhouses, one labeled, *Boys*, the other, *Girls*. Beyond that was a huge cottonwood tree. Beneath the tree there was a wooden rail to which were tied the saddle horses some of the children rode to school. Molly Teplin's buggy sat nearby, its shafts resting on the ground.

On the schoolhouse roof there was a small bell cupola. And on the south side of the school there were several swings.

A low buzz of voices came from the open windows of the school. Inside, Molly Teplin left her younger class and stepped into the room that held the older children, those from the fifth grade on up.

These were the most restless ones, she thought, and their restlessness, normal this time of year, had not been helped by Slade Teplin's arrival in Cottonwood Springs.

She had missed Tommy Schilling and Tony Sanchez earlier, immediately after first recess. Now, she made a mental count of the others. All were here. But she was sure more would be missing after lunch.

Thinking of Slade, back again, stirred conflicting feelings in her. She could not help remembering the first few months of their marriage. And now, with so many years betwen the present and those first months, she realized something she had never realized before. She had not married Slade because she was in love with him. She had felt sorry for him and had mistaken the feeling of pity for love. She had believed him when he'd told her he had been forced into using his gun as a way of life. She had believed him when he said he had never used the gun for pay, nor killed except in self defense.

She did not believe it now. She'd had five years to think about it, to remember, to see Slade as he really was, not as her young idealism had made him seem. She knew he was a killer and she knew he would always be just that. She knew as well that some core of evil must lie within his mind, or he would not be what he was.

This morning, facing her class with hands that trembled in spite of herself, she admitted something else. She was afraid of Slade. She was afraid of what he would do to Johnny Yoder if he found out Johnny had been seeing her. She was even afraid of what Slade might do to her.

He was here, now, in Cottonwood Springs. He was here, after five long years. The morning might pass without him seeking her out. But at lunch time . . . she knew she'd see him then.

She put her hands behind her to hide their trembling. She said, "I want all of you to spend the next half hour writing a composition. The subject will be up to you. And I want no talking. Do you understand?"

Their faces were young and eager, and she had the vague impression that they were more respectful than usual today. *And why not*, she thought bitterly. *They know I am Slade Teplin's wife. They admire him — think he's some kind of hero for what he's done. Part of the luster has rubbed off on me simply because I am his wife.*

His wife. The word implied many things, all of which seemed unbearable to Molly. The intimacy of living together in the same house, sharing the same bed at night. She felt her face grow pale. She should have listened to Johnny months ago. She should have divorced Slade then. But even then, she realized, she had feared him. She had feared what he might do when he got the news.

Johnny. Her face softened as she thought of him, as she pictured him in her mind. He was all the things Slade would never be. A man who was not dependent upon reputation and skill with a gun for confidence in his own manhood. A man who was not afraid, even of Slade, even of Slade's appalling speed with his gun.

Johnny would face Slade without a qualm. She felt, suddenly, as cold as ice. It must not happen. She must not permit it to happen. Because if it did, Johnny would be killed.

Again she tortured herself with the question, "Why did he come back?"

She turned and left the room. She went outside onto the narrow porch. The sun beating against her felt good but it failed to thaw the ice that seemed to lie like a chunk within her chest. Had Slade come back for her? Was it as simple as that?

It was possible, of course. But she did not believe it. Why should he come back for her now? Why, after five long years? He had not even written her. He had sent no money for her support. He seemed to have forgotten her.

But if he had not come back for her, then why had he returned? Was it possible he had changed? Was it possible he was weary of the kind of life he led? Was he seeking peace and a normal life?

That too was possible, she thought. Slade had been warped and twisted by his early life. He had learned to hate the town. But the years can cool even the most burning hatred. Time can ease even the most painful of wounds.

She stared toward the town, half expecting to see him walking along the street toward the school.

Impatient with herself, she turned and reentered the building. She passed down the aisle in the room containing the older children, collecting their papers. She glanced at the titles as she did. More than half of them had titles like, "Slade Teplin, My Teacher's Husband," or "Our Town's Hero."

She wanted to tell them that Slade was no

hero, that no one is who takes sixteen lives in personal duels that have no sense or reason to justify them. She wanted to remind them of the Lord's commandment, "Thou shall not kill." She wanted to tell them what Slade really was, a man filled with hatred for humanity who fed his hatred on human life.

But she knew she could not, because it would be a contradiction they would not understand. She was Mrs. Slade Teplin. She had married him.

No. She couldn't tell them about Slade. But perhaps their parents could.

She was tempted, suddenly, to dismiss school for the day. She didn't want the children to be here when Slade came. She didn't want them to see her with him.

She resisted the idea almost frantically. Letting the children out would simply be giving them permission to hang around on Main Street or wherever Slade was for the rest of the day. If there was trouble, one or more of the children might possibly be in the line of fire and be hurt or killed.

Trouble. The only two in town who might have trouble would be Slade and Johnny. And it would be trouble over her.

Letting school out was impossible, she

thought. But so was staying here, tortured by her thoughts, unconsciously listening for the sound of gunfire in the town.

What would she do if she did hear guns, she asked herself. And she knew the answer almost immediately. She'd run. She'd run as though the devil pursued her straight toward the sounds. She wouldn't stop running until she knew . . . if Johnny was hurt . . . if Johnny had been killed.

A hand was up in the back of the room but it was several moments before she saw it. When she did see it, she said, "Karl. What is it?"

"You reckon he'll kill Johnny Yoder, Mrs. Teplin? You reckon that's what he come back for?"

"Came back for," she corrected automatically. Then she said quickly, "Of course not, Karl. Whatever gave you that idea?"

"It's what my pa said was goin' to happen. As sure as God made little green apples."

"Your father's wrong this time, Karl. Nothing of the sort is going to happen. Now sit down. I'm going to write some problems on the blackboard. I want them done before the bell rings for lunch."

She turned her back and went to the board. She wrote out several arithmetic problems with the chalk.

She had to force herself to concentrate. All the time she was writing she was hearing the guns, seeing Johnny Yoder fall, seeing him limp and lifeless on the ground afterward.

When she turned away from the board, her mind was made up. No longer did she hesitate. She would go back to Slade. If he wanted her, she would go back.

She heard the smaller children chattering and went out onto the porch. Her heart seemed to stand still. What would she say to him? What could she say, after all these years?

But it was not Slade. It was Johnny Yoder, riding up on his brown gelding.

Molly felt the tension drain out of her. She felt almost weak. She made a tremulous smile and stepped down off the porch. Johnny dismounted.

His face was grave and filled with concern. He said, "You ought to dismiss school and go on home."

"I'm all right, Johnny."

"You don't look all right. Don't let him upset you this way." He peered at her closely.

"You haven't seen him, have you?"

She shook her head wordlessly. How, she wondered with desperation, could she make Johnny understand what she meant to do? She wouldn't, she realized, unless she could convince him that she loved Slade and wanted to go back to him. It wouldn't be easy, because Johnny had known her for a year. But a man has pride, she thought. She would attack and destroy Johnny's pride.

She looked away from him, suddenly no longer able to meet his eyes. Destroy his pride or let him lose his life. It wasn't much of a choice, she thought bitterly.

She whispered, "You'll have to go now. The children are hard enough to manage this morning as it is. Besides, he might come and I don't want him to find you here."

"Why not? Maybe it'd be a good thing all around if we just had this thing out now, once and for all."

Molly glanced up at him. It was difficult to meet his eyes, but she held them steadily by sheer force of will. "Please, Johnny. Please. Not now. Not here. Not ever."

Johnny said fiercely, "I won't let him have you!"

"Maybe he doesn't even want me, Johnny.

Maybe it's just a short visit. He might not try to see me at all."

"He'll see you. And you'd better be thinking about what you're going to say to him." Johnny's face was flushed with anger and his eyes snapped with it. But it was gone almost as quickly as it had been born. He said softly, "I'm sorry. This is as hard on you as it is on me. I just want to help."

"Then go now, Johnny. I'll stop by the sheriff's office on my way home from school."

He glanced at the windows of the school and she knew he wanted to kiss her but would not in front of all the children. He grinned. "They don't miss much, do they?"

"They don't miss anything."

He mounted his horse, sat there looking at her worriedly for a moment, then turned the horse and rode away. She watched him until he turned the corner onto Main and disappeared from sight.

Wearily she turned and went back inside the school. There was a great scramble as the younger children returned hurriedly to their seats.

Time dragged endlessly. Half a dozen times before noon, Molly went to the door and stared out. But at last the hands of the clock pointed to twelve and she rang the noon bell. The children streamed out, some carrying lard-pail lunch buckets, some to mount their horses and head for home, some to walk toward home. In five minutes the schoolyard was virtually deserted except for half-a-dozen children sitting beneath the huge cottonwood.

And then Molly saw him, standing beside a cottonwood in the yard nearest the school, about a hundred yards away.

She walked toward him, no welcome in her eyes, no welcome in her heart, but preferring to talk to him well out of the children's hearing.

He was dressed in black and wore a narrow-brimmed black hat. The holstered gun, hanging at his side, looked bigger than it ever had before. She fixed her eyes on it with a kind of fascination, thinking that this gun, in this man's hand, had killed sixteen men and would kill more.

There was no more welcome in Slade's eyes than there was in hers. There was a mocking, unpleasant smile on his mouth. He said, "Well. If it isn't my devoted wife."

She raised her eyes from his gun and met his glance. She felt her face flushing and it angered her. She wanted to be ice-cold with him, composed and self assured. Yet before his mocking smile her composure evaporated like dew in the morning sun. She said lifelessly, "Hello, Slade."

"What kind of welcome is that, after five long years?"

"It's more than you deserve."

"Why? Because you've found another man?"

"That has nothing to do with it. You've been gone five years. You deserted me. You haven't written in all that time."

"But you're still my wife."

"Yes, Slade, I'm still your wife."

He stood there staring down at her for a long, long time. Molly somehow felt unclean under his scrutiny. At last, unable to stand his silent staring any longer, she cried, "Why did you have to come back? Why? What is it you want?"

"What's comin' to me, maybe. Maybe that's what I came home to get."

"What is coming to you, Slade?"

He stood there silently, refusing to answer her. Then, without a word, he turned and stalked down the street toward town.

She watched him go, her face bloodless. She still didn't know what he meant to do. She had a feeling she wouldn't know until it was too late.

Chapter 6

After leaving Molly at the school, Johnny Yoder rode back toward the sheriff's office. He was furious and there was a murderous scowl on his face. But there was something cold within his chest, something he recognized as fear.

He turned the corner onto Main. Suddenly he found it hard to believe that Slade Teplin had been in Cottonwood Springs for only three hours. It seemed as though the man had been here for days.

This was Wednesday, but Main Street looked like a busy Saturday. Rigs were drawn up before the stores all along the street. Ranchers that Johnny seldom saw except on Saturday nodded and spoke to him as he rode down the street.

In front of the Ace High and the Emporia, horses were racked solidly. From both saloons came the steady buzz of voices.

Johnny halted in front of the Emporia. He crowded his horse in at the already crowded rack and looped the reins around the rail. He went inside.

He didn't really want a drink. It was too early in the day for him. But he sometimes had a beer just before dinner. Besides, he wanted to be seen. He didn't want tongues wagging any more than they already were.

The place was packed. Johnny heard Slade's name half a dozen times as he pushed patiently toward the bar. He reached it and crowded in. "Gimme a beer, Sam."

"Sure, Johnny." Sam Riordan filled a heavy mug and slid it along the bar. Johnny put a nickel down. Sam wiped his forehead with a sleeve and came to stand in front of him. "I wish there'd be a Slade Teplin come to town every day. I ain't done so much on a weekday since the trail drives stopped coming years ago."

"Then it's not all bad, is it, Sam?"

"Nope." Sam leaned across the bar, lowering his voice. "I'd keep an eye on Cal Reeder if I was you. He's makin' some pretty strong fight talk."

"About trying Slade? He was talking that way this morning, but I thought it was only talk. You think he'd really do it?"

"I don't know. Maybe he'll shut up when Slade comes in but I wouldn't count on it. He's been drinking. And the more he drinks the wilder he talks."

"Where is he?"

"Over there."

Johnny followed Sam's pointing finger with his eyes. He saw Cal Reeder, surrounded by about a dozen men, over in a corner of the place. Cal was talking. His face was flushed. Johnny nodded, finished his beer and pushed patiently through the crowd.

He reached the group in time to hear Cal Reeder say, "It don't make sense, that's all. Every one of them sixteen men sure as hell wasn't a gunfighter. Maybe he even shot some of 'em in the back."

"You better not say that to Slade, Cal. In fact you'd better not say it at all."

"Why not? I ain't afraid of him."

Johnny pushed to a place in front of him. "You'd ought to be even if you're not. I can tell you what several of those sixteen men were. Kids just like you with more guts than sense. Now finish your drink and go on home."

"Go home hell! I ain't leavin' here. This is the biggest thing that's happened in this town in years."

Johnny looked at him sourly. "It'll be bigger if you don't shut that big mouth of yours."

Cal laughed nastily. "You might be scared of him, Johnny, but I sure ain't. He's only a man, ain't he?"

"Yeah. He's only a man. But he's alive and the sixteen who faced him are dead. You think on that."

He stared at Cal's face, fixing Cal's eyes with his own steady glance. Cal started to say something but Johnny said harshly, "Shut up! You've said too much already. Go on home if you want to stay alive."

He turned his back and pushed toward the door. There was silence behind him for a moment, then he heard Cal say loudly, "I still say I'm right. Just because Slade's killed sixteen men don't mean he's some kind of a god. He's only a man."

Johnny heard another voice behind him, and recognized it as Phil Regan's voice. "Why don't you prove that, Cal? Why don't you take him on?"

Disgust and exasperation washed over Johnny. Phil Regan was all Cal Reeder needed. With Phil to egg him on he just might be fool enough. . . .

But there was nothing Johnny could do

71

about it. He couldn't *make* Cal go home. He couldn't jail him either. He wasn't drunk and he wasn't disturbing the peace.

He reached the door and stepped outside. He almost collided with John McCracken on the walk. McCracken stopped. "Hello, Johnny."

"Hello, Mr. McCracken."

Everyone in town called McCracken mister. Johnny thought wryly that his wife probably did too. McCracken was that kind of man.

He was tall, as tall as Johnny was. He was heavier, a bulky, powerful kind of heaviness. His hair was gray and he wore a trimmed beard and mustache.

He was dressed in a dark business suit. A gold chain stretched across his vest from pocket to pocket.

McCracken made a small, frosty smile. "You ever seen anything like this, Johnny?"

Johnny shook his head. McCracken snorted disgustedly, "A damned Roman holiday. I hope he doesn't stay here long."

Johnny said, "This'll wear off, even if he does." He wanted to mention Barney, but he did not. He wanted to ask how Slade's return was going to affect Barney's job with the bank. Barney needed that job. He needed the respect that went along with it.

McCracken snorted disgustedly and moved on down the street toward the bank.

Johnny fished the Bull Durham sack from his pocket and made a cigarette. He lighted it. Glancing up, he saw Slade Teplin walking down Main from the direction of the school. Behind Slade by perhaps a hundred feet, came two boys he recognized as Tommy Schilling and Tony Sanchez.

Again he could not help noticing the way Slade Teplin moved — like a cat, stalking a bird. That was the impression, yet it was not as plain as that.

He had intended returning to the sheriff's office, but he knew he couldn't now. Not until Slade had reached the Emporia, if that was where he was headed. If he left right now it would look as if he were avoiding Slade.

So he waited, tension and dislike building in him, and kept his glance steadily on Slade as the man approached.

How good Slade was, he couldn't guess. Perhaps, in a sense, Cal Reeder was right. All of the sixteen Slade had killed probably had not been particularly fast. But Johnny was also sure, in his own mind, that Slade had not hand-picked them because they weren't fast. Slade, he was certain, took them as they came.

Slade saw Johnny and stared at him steadily as he approached. Johnny didn't speak or even nod. He returned the stare impassively, but he knew the anger he felt was showing in his eyes.

Slade stopped immediately in front of him. "You must be the deputy – the one who's been seeing my wife." His voice was flat, almost as expressionless as his face.

Johnny said coldly, "I'm the one." He knew, even as he said it, that his tone conveyed the defiant, unspoken question, "What are you going to do about it?"

Slade stared at him fixedly for several more moments. Then he said, "We'll talk on that, deputy, but not right now."

Johnny said, "Any time."

Slade went into the saloon. Johnny's whole body was tense. He had half expected Slade to challenge him, he realized. He felt himself relax and suddenly felt almost weak.

Behind him, as Slade entered the Emporia, the noise quieted instantly. A moment before a steady buzz of voices had emanated from the place. Now the silence was complete.

He turned his head and glanced over the swinging doors. Slade was crossing the room toward the bar. A path had opened for him almost magically. There were no friendly greetings. There was nothing but silent awe.

In spite of his anger, his resentment toward the man, Johnny suddenly felt sorry for him. Slade Teplin lived in a lonely, solitary world. He had no friends. He was not a part of the strange but sometimes wonderful mixture of humanity.

Slade ordered a drink and Sam Riordan served him silently. Johnny wondered where Barney was. He glanced down toward the bank and searched the street with his glance but he did not see Barney anywhere.

The Ace-High was emptying and those who had been there were streaming down the street toward the Emporia. Johnny moved aside to let them in. They crowded past him and into the saloon. They filled the doorway and packed the area immediately in front of the swinging doors.

Suddenly, loud and plain in the silence, came a shout from inside the saloon. "Hey! You! Slade Teplin!"

There was a moment's silence. No one seemed to breathe. Recognizing that voice, Johnny slammed into the crowd in front of the Emporia and fought his way toward the door.

It was like fighting a yielding wall. He could only push so far and then his progress stopped. Using his hands, he began frantically to shove men aside. He yelled, "God damn it, let me through!"

He still had not reached the doors, still could not see inside when he heard the voice again, "I hear you've killed sixteen men. How many of the sixteen did you shoot in the back?"

Now there was sound inside the Emporia, but it was not the sound of voices. It was the sound of pushing, crowding. It was the sound of men frantically trying to get out of the line of fire.

Johnny heard Slade's voice, just as he reached the doors. "Go on home boy and forget it."

"Forget it hell! Unless you're too damned yellow to fight."

Johnny was fighting frantically. He roared, "Cal! Shut your goddamn mouth!"

Cal shouted, "Go on, gunfighter! Draw and let's see how fast you really are!"

Johnny was pushed back bodily from the door, pushed by a solid wall of frantic humanity, men trying to get out of the Emporia before the guns came out. He kept on fighting, flinging men aside so violently that some of them fell. But for every one he flung away, another crowded out to take his place. He heard Slade's flat, expressionless voice, "All right, sonny. Any time you're ready you just go ahead."

Johnny knew he'd never get inside – not in time to stop what was happening. Cal didn't have a chance. He roared, "Cal! Listen to me! Don't touch your gun!"

He reached the doors and got a glimpse of the pair over the heads of those still trying to crowd out of the saloon. There was an open space between Teplin and Cal. Behind Cal there was another open space in which no men stood.

He didn't see Sam Riordan at all and guessed Riordan had ducked down behind the bar. And then he saw Cal move.

His eyes, so briefly on Cal, missed Slade Teplin's movement altogether, so fast were they. But he saw the flash of Teplin's gun and he heard its obscene roar. He saw the cloud of powdersmoke that billowed out in front of it.

Cal's gun never fired at all, but it was in his hand, raising, as Slade's bullet took him in the chest.

He was driven back by the terrible force of the heavy slug. He slammed against a table and it overturned. He tripped on it, still staggering back, and sprawled over the overturned table, hanging there like a grotesque, broken doll. A red stain began to spread across his white shirt-front.

Slade Teplin holstered his gun. He looked at Johnny's face over the heads of the crowd, and his eyes held a strange glow, a fixed intensity. He said, "You saw that, deputy. He drew before I did."

Now, too late, the crowd parted to let Johnny through. He ignored Teplin and walked to where Cal lay, still draped across the overturned table.

Cal was dead. His face was relaxed, peaceful. His eyes were open but they were expressionless. He looked like a boy — like he was maybe sixteen or seventeen.

Johnny turned angrily. He glared at Slade for a moment, wanting to say so many things, knowing how useless it would be. Nothing he could say would bring Cal Reeder back. Nothing he could say would have any effect on Slade.

He stalked to the door and went outside. The noonday sun beat down hotly into the street. In spite of it, Johnny's body felt as cold as ice.

He heard a scream, and glanced up the

street. He saw Molly, running, holding up her skirts so that she would not trip on them.

He ran toward her, and half a block from the Emporia reached her and caught her in his arms.

She was sobbing uncontrollably. Her body trembled violently.

Johnny held her close for a long, long time, until her trembling lessened, until her sobs stopped. She drew back her head and looked up at him, face white, tears streaming down her cheeks. Her voice was almost hysterical, "I was listening . . . I heard a shot and I thought it was you! Oh my God, Johnny, I thought it was you!"

She pulled away from him suddenly, her glance fixed on something behind him. She whispered, "Who was it, Johnny? Who?"

Johnny turned his head. Slade Teplin was standing on the walk in front of the Emporia. He was staring at them. Suddenly he turned and went back into the saloon.

Johnny said, "Cal Reeder, Molly. It was Cal."

Molly said in a strained, tight voice, "I wish he was dead. God forgive me, Johnny, I wish Slade was in his grave!"

Chapter 7

There was a lot of confusion back there at the Emporia. Arch Schilling came striding along the street from the jail. He went into the Emporia. Johnny looked down at Molly's tearful face. "I'll walk you back to the school."

She shook her head. "No. I'm all right now." Turning, she glimpsed Tommy Schilling and Tony Sanchez peering out from a narrow passageway between two stores. She called, "Tommy, Tony! Come here this minute!"

They hesitated a moment between obeying and running away. Then, sheepishly, the pair shuffled across the dusty street. Molly said, "Get back to school this instant! Both of you!"

The boys were no longer in the grip of hero worship. Both of them were thoroughly scared. They ducked their heads and shuffled away toward the school. Molly glanced at Johnny. Her eyes were still red from weeping and they were filled with fear. "Johnny. Don't let him . . . don't get into a fight with him."

"All right, Molly. Now stop worrying."

She smiled wanly. She looked at his face lingeringly, her smile fading. Then without a word she turned and walked back in the direction of the school.

Johnny returned to the Emporia. He reached it as a couple of men carried Cal outside.

There was shock in the faces of the onlookers. In some there was outrage, or anger. One man said, as Arch Schilling came out, "This is terrible, Sheriff. It's a damned disgrace. What are you going to do about it?"

Arch didn't bother to reply. The two men carried the body down the street toward Jim Hawkins' Furniture and Undertaking Parlor.

Johnny looked around for Slade, but Slade had disappeared. Arch glanced at him and said, "Somebody's got to do it, Johnny. It might as well be you."

"Do what?"

"Ride out to Reeder's place. Tell Ward what's happened to Cal."

Johnny stared at him, hesitating. He didn't want to ride out to Reeder's place. It would take him three hours, going and coming, even if he hurried all the way. A lot could happen here in three hours.

He said, "Arch, you know how that's going to look. Like I was running away from him."

Arch's face showed sudden anger. "Who the hell cares how it looks? Somebody's got to do it."

"Then get someone else. I want to stay right here."

Arch opened his mouth to speak, then closed it with a snap. His glance went beyond Johnny and Johnny turned his head to follow. He saw Barney Teplin coming along Main from the direction of his house.

Barney was drunk. He was weaving, staggering. He banged up against a storefront and nearly fell. Recovering, he came diagonally across the street. Arch said under his breath, "For Christ's sake! I was afraid of this."

Leaving Johnny, he crossed the street, intercepting Barney in the middle. Johnny followed him. Arch took one of Barney's arms and Johnny took the other. Barney protested drunkenly but the two of them turned him and headed him back toward home again. Arch said, "You don't want any more, Barney. Come on. We'll walk you home."

As he turned, Johnny got a glimpse of John McCracken watching from the doorway of the bank. He suddenly felt a little sick to his stomach.

Slade had been here only a little more than three hours. Already he had killed a man. He had, somehow, caused his father to fall off the wagon he'd been on almost ten years. He had jeopardized his father's job and his self-respect.

Barney walked between them unprotestingly until they reached his house. At the front gate, he pulled away from them violently. He mumbled, "I'm all right. Lemme alone."

Arch caught his arm. "We'll help you in."

Barney flung his arm off so violently that he staggered and fell in a heap. "No! You can't come in. I'm all right, dammit. Now lemme alone!"

Arch looked at Johnny helplessly. Then his jaw firmed out. "I'll be damned if I'm going to leave him out here. Come on, we'll take him inside."

They hauled Barney to his feet, still protesting violently. As they approached the porch, Barney began to fight but now they had him firmly between them. They dragged him up onto the porch and through the front door.

Once inside, Barney suddenly ceased to fight. He began to weep brokenly, drunkenly.

Johnny stared around at the wreckage of the room. He stared at the broken shotgun lying in the middle of the floor.

Arch's voice was soft, but it was just like ice. "Who did this, Barney? Slade?"

"No! I did it. You know how I am when I get drunk."

"Yeah. I know how you are, Barney. You wouldn't hurt a fly."

Johnny didn't miss the bottle lying unbroken in a corner of the room. There was still a little whisky in the bottle. He also saw the two glasses lying near to it. One had been broken but the other was whole.

Barney stood swaying in the center of the room. Tears streamed unheeded down his cheeks. Arch said, very softly, very gently, "Go to bed, Barney."

Barney turned, as meekly as a child. He went into his bedroom off the parlor and Johnny heard the bedsprings creak as he fell limply across the bed.

Arch looked helplessly around the room a

moment, then turned and went outside. Johnny crossed to the bedroom door and peered in at Barney. Barney was already asleep, his mouth open, his cheek still wet with tears.

Johnny went out, closing the door softly behind him. He walked along silently with Arch, not speaking until they were half a block away. Then he breathed, "The son-of-a-bitch! The dirty son-of-a-bitch!"

"Yeah. Now get your horse and ride out to Ward Reeder's place. And don't give me any back-talk."

"What are you going to do about Slade?"

Arch was silent for several moments. At last he said, "Do? What the hell can I do? Barney won't sign a complaint. There are twenty or thirty witnesses to the shooting and they all say Cal started it and drew first."

Johnny's mind was clicking rapidly. School let out at three-thirty. It couldn't be much later than twelve-thirty now. If he hurried, he could at least be back from Reeder's place by the time school let out. He'd even have a little extra leeway because Molly never left the school building until four.

And maybe Arch was right. Maybe he should get out of town this afternoon. His own anger, his own outrage was growing steadily. He was rapidly approaching the point where he'd do something about Slade himself.

They reached Main Street. Arch said, "I'm going to talk to John McCracken for a minute. You get your horse and go."

Johnny untied his horse from the rail in front of the Emporia. The place was still crowded. The conversation was excited — about the shooting that had taken place such a short time before.

Johnny mounted and turned downstreet. Then, changing his mind, he reversed directions and touched his horse's sides with his heels. The animal broke into a lope.

Johnny wheeled around the corner and headed for the school. No use letting Molly worry about him all afternoon uselessly, he thought. If she knew he wasn't even in town, she wouldn't be so likely to make any rash decisions out of concern for him.

There was a small group of children playing on the swings. Tommy and Tony sat on the porch steps, talking in subdued tones. Molly heard him and came out, to stand with a hand raised to shield her eyes from the glare of the sun.

Johnny didn't dismount. He said, "I'm

going out to Ward Reeder's place and tell him about Cal. I'll be back before school lets out."

The relief that came into her eyes made him feel warm inside. He said firmly, "It will be all right, Molly. It will be all right."

She nodded, but she didn't speak. He turned and rode away, circling the town instead of riding through it.

The sun was hot on his back. The sky was still a flawless blue, but now a few fluffy clouds floated in it like puffs of smoke. He let his horse slow to a steady trot, an uncomfortable gait for a man but an easy one for the horse and one that covered the miles fast.

He dreaded the errand that lay ahead of him. He dreaded telling Ward Reeder that his only son was dead. But it was like Arch had said. Someone had to do it and it might as well be him.

He came abreast of the butte, several miles to his left, and passed on beyond it. He was heading almost directly north.

He continued his horse's steady gait for a little more than an hour before he saw the distant cluster of buildings ahead of him. He rode for yet another twenty minutes before he reached the place.

Ward Reeder's ranch was one of the biggest around Cottonwood Springs. Reeder ran almost a thousand cattle. He had seven sections of deeded land. He hired two men and kept them busy from dawn until dark.

Johnny halted his horse in the yard between the house and barn. He dismounted reluctantly. He hoped Ward was here. He didn't want to take time to ride all over the countryside looking for him.

He breathed a soft sigh of relief as Ward emerged from the barn and yelled, "Hey, Johnny! Here I am. What the hell brings you 'way out here?"

Johnny led his horse toward the man. Ward Reeder was about fifty, he guessed. He was stocky, broad and powerful, almost the exact opposite in build and temperament as Cal had been.

Reeder asked, "Did Slade Teplin come in on the train?"

Johnny nodded.

"How's he look?"

Johnny said, "I didn't know him before. He looks . . . well, like I'd have expected him to I guess."

Reeder's glance sharpened suddenly. "What'd you come out here for? What the hell's the matter with you?"

Johnny swallowed hard. He said, "It's Cal. He —"

"What about Cal? Damn you, what about Cal?"

"He's dead."

For an instant Ward Reeder was silent. Then he grabbed Johnny by both arms and shook him. "You're a liar! You're a goddamn liar!"

Johnny didn't resist. He shook his head silently.

Reeder roared, "Quit lyin' to me! Quit it! Why'd you really come out?"

"To tell you Cal was dead. Arch sent me out."

Reeder released him. He stepped back, breathing hard. He stared at the ground for a moment. His big, broad hands were trembling. So were his thick, solid knees. He looked up. "Who did it? How'd it happen?"

"Slade. Cal forced a fight with him."

"You see it?" Ward's voice was lifeless.

Johnny nodded. "I saw it. I was trying to get through the crowd. I yelled at Cal not to touch his gun but he wouldn't listen to me. He tried, but . . . well, he never even fired."

"Where is he? I mean where's his . . ."

Ward swallowed and said in a voice that almost choked, "Where's his body at?"

"Jim Hawkins' place. Arch had a couple of men take him there." Johnny stared at him silently for a moment. He said, "I'm sorry, Ward."

"Sure, Johnny. Sure." Ward stood there uncertainly for several moments. Then he muttered, "That goddamn kid! That goddamn stupid kid! I told him. I told him a thousand times . . ."

Johnny said softly, "Can I get your horse for you, Ward? I'll ride in with you."

"No. I'll get him, Johnny. You go on ahead. I'll catch up."

Johnny mounted and turned his horse toward town. He rode out at a walk. He had gone no more than a quarter mile when he heard Reeder coming along behind.

Reeder wore a six-shooter. There was a rifle jammed into his saddle boot. His face was grim and cold.

Johnny knew the thoughts that were going through Reeder's head. He knew what Reeder meant to do.

He'd face Slade Teplin over the killing of his son. And he'd be killed himself. He'd be number eighteen on Slade Teplin's list.

Someone had to do something, he thought

miserably to himself. Someone had to stop the inevitable, tightening circle of death.

The miles passed beneath their horses' hoofs. Johnny's anger mounted steadily. There was nothing he could do. There was nothing anyone could do.

Chapter 8

It was exactly three-fifteen when Johnny and Ward Reeder thundered across the plank bridge spanning Cottonwood Creek. Arch Schilling must have been watching for them from the jail because no sooner had they entered Main at the lower end than Johnny saw Arch coming down the street on foot.

Arch stopped and stood in the center of the street in front of Regan's Livery Barn. Johnny drew his horse to a halt. For a moment he thought Ward would ride past, but something about Arch's hard old eyes stopped him. Ward glowered down at the sheriff. "Save your breath, Arch. He killed my boy."

"And he'll kill you too if you give him half a chance."

Ward's heavy face held more bitterness than Johnny had ever seen in it. "What would *you* do, Arch? Let him get away with it? Cal never had a chance against him and you damn well know he didn't."

"Think you'll have a better one?"

Ward's eyes blazed. His mouth was a slash in his anger-reddened face. He said, "Sheriff, there's something dirty wrong with this. Slade murdered Cal. You know it and I know it. Now you tell me I'll have to let it go or die myself. Well maybe I won't do either one. Maybe I'll get Slade some other way."

"It'll be murder if you do. I'll have to arrest you for it."

Johnny studied Arch's face. It was filled with anger at the injustice of what he had just said. It was filled with helpless outrage at a situation where Slade could kill but Ward could not. Arch said, "Ward, I know it isn't right, but I can't change it and neither can you. It's a hold-over from the dueling code and until the laws are changed, it'll stay that way. But some day the Slade Teplin's are going to have to answer for every man they kill, self-defense or not."

Ward glowered for several moments, finally grumbling, "That's a big help to me right now!"

Arch didn't reply. Ward said, "I want

to see my boy."

"He's at Jim Hawkins' place."

Ward touched his horse's sides with his heels and moved on past. Johnny held his horse motionless. Arch stood spread-legged in the street and watched as Ward rode angrily away. He turned his head and looked helplessly up at Johnny.

Johnny asked, "Where's Slade now?"

"He took a room at the hotel. He's been there all afternoon."

Johnny glanced past him up the street. There were fewer rigs tied along the street and less than half as many saddle horses as there had been earlier. He said, "Looks like the crowd's thinned out."

"Yeah. A lot of 'em went home. The streets get empty when there's a mad dog loose."

Johnny dismounted and walked toward the jail, pacing Arch. He asked, "Isn't there *anything* we can do?"

"Not one goddamn thing. Unless we can get Barney to sign a complaint."

"Think he'd be sober now?"

"Might. Why don't you ride over there and see?"

Johnny nodded. He pulled his heavy silver watch from his pocket and glanced at it. It was almost three-thirty, but he could spare fifteen minutes to talk to Barney and still get to the school before Molly left.

He swung to the back of his horse. He glanced at the hotel as he went past. The usual number of loafers were there on the porch. They watched him go by almost furtively. None of them spoke.

Johnny turned the corner and headed for Barney's place, hurrying, thinking of Molly now, and anxious to be done with this.

Ward Reeder dismounted in front of Jim Hawkins' store. He looped his horse's reins around the rail with hands that trembled violently.

He felt stunned, unbelieving yet. It didn't seem possible that Cal was dead. Heavily he crossed the worn boardwalk and went inside.

The front part of the store was filled with furniture. There was a distinctive smell of wood and cloth about the place. Jim Hawkins, an elderly man with snow-white hair, came from the back room to see who had come in.

He called, "Back here, Ward."

Ward walked down the aisle. Hawkins' gaunt, lined face was sympathetic. "I'm sorry, Ward. It's a terrible thing."

Ward grunted noncommittally. He shouldered past Hawkins into the small room at the rear.

It was a barren room. Over at one side there was a bed. Cal's body lay on it, a sheet drawn over his head. Nearby there were two straight-backed chairs.

Ward crossed the room. He knew his face was bloodless. There was a feeling of nausea in his stomach. His hand shook almost uncontrollably as he lifted the sheet and pulled it away from Cal's face. It was white, pasty-colored. Cal's eyes were closed.

Ward dropped the sheet. He stumbled to one of the straight-backed chairs and sank into it. He whispered, "God! Oh Holy God!"

Hawkins was silent for a long, long time. At last he asked, "What do you want to do about funeral arrangements, Ward? Shall I get Orville Newcomb? Do you want the funeral in the church?"

Ward stared at him numbly, and Hawkins repeated his questions gently. Ward nodded finally, and Hawkins asked, "Is tomorrow all right? About ten?"

Ward nodded again. Almost as though speaking to himself, he said, "He wasn't a bad kid, Jim. Wild is all. Ranching never interested him. Not enough excitement, I guess. But I thought it would wear out. I thought he'd get enough of drinkin' and hellin' around and packin' that damned gun."

"He would have, Ward. If . . ." Hawkins stopped suddenly.

Ward Reeder finished the sentence for him. "If he'd lived. If that damn Slade Teplin had stayed away."

He sat there for several moments more, staring blankly at the floor between his feet. Hawkins silently withdrew, closing the door softly behind him.

As the door closed, a tremor shook Reeder's stocky frame. A single, gusty sob escaped his lips.

He straightened then. He brushed impatiently at his eyes with the back of one work-roughened hand. He stood up.

Maybe he couldn't kill Slade Teplin, he thought. He couldn't outdraw the man and if he killed him any other way he'd have to stand trial for it. But there was something he could do. He could make Slade Teplin wish he'd never come back here. He could make him wish he'd never seen Cal.

He crossed the room and opened the door. Hawkins was waiting silently outside of it.

Ward asked heavily, "Jim, will you take care of things? The grave and all?"

Hawkins nodded. Ward went past him to the front of the store.

He stood there, inside the door for a moment, studying the sheriff's office and jail across the street. He did not see Arch.

He went out, untied his horse and mounted quickly. He turned the horse toward the Emporia up the street.

Reaching it, he dismounted and tied the horse. He went in.

The place was far from full, but there were maybe fifteen or twenty men. Ward went to the bar. Sam Riordan came to stand in front of him, his face soberly sympathetic. He said, "Ward, I'm sorry. I . . ."

Ward asked harshly, "Where is he now?"

"Cal? Over at Jim Hawkins' place."

"I mean Slade. Where is he?"

"Ward, don't do it. Don't be a fool. He'll kill you too."

Ward reached suddenly across the bar. He seized Sam by the shirtfront and yanked him close against the bar. His voice was savage. "Where is he? Damn you!"

Sam said, "He took a room at the hotel. He's been there all afternoon."

Ward released him. He turned, as though

to leave, then suddenly swung around again. Deliberately, he reached down and unbuckled his gun and belt. He laid it on the bar. "Keep this for me. I'll be back for it."

Relief washed across Sam Riordan's scared face. He breathed, "That's smart, Ward. For a minute there I . . ."

Ward stalked out of the saloon. Half a dozen of the men got up and followed him. He walked toward the hotel, the six following a dozen yards behind. A moment later another man came out of the Emporia and hurried toward the jail.

Ward reached the hotel and went inside. He crossed the huge, cool lobby to the desk. Alf Holloway started to speak, but Ward cut him short. "Which room's he in?"

"I can't . . . I'm not . . ." Alf's young eyes were terrified.

"Which room, damn you?" Reeder roared.

"I . . ." Alf tried to hold Reeder's glance and failed. He mumbled, "Seventeen, Mr. Reeder. But . . ."

Ward turned and strode across the lobby to the stairs. He took them two at a time. At the head of the stairs, he turned right and hurried along the hall. He stopped in front of seventeen.

Here, he stood for a moment, letting

anger rise in him, letting it grow to an almost intolerable pitch. Then he hammered on the door.

He heard the creak of bedsprings inside the room. He heard footsteps coming toward the door. It opened and Slade Teplin stood there looking at him, his gun in his hand and pointing straight at Ward Reeder's chest.

Ward felt the muscles in his arms twitching. His chest felt tight. There was a lightness in his brain. He growled, "You son-of-a-bitch! You dirty son-of-a-bitch! You killed my boy!"

Slade's eyes were glazed with sudden awakening. Ward bawled, "You bastard! You can kill a man and then come here and go to sleep? What kind of stinkin' animal are you anyway?"

"Get out of here before I blow your head off."

"Go ahead. You just go ahead. You'll hang for it because I haven't got a gun. Take a look. I haven't got a gun. I left it at the Emporia."

A shadow of doubt crossed Slade Teplin's face. Ward said softly, "Put it away or shoot it. Make up your mind and make it up right now."

Slade lowered the gun. As he did, Ward plunged through the door, striking him with his shoulder and knocking him halfway across the room. Slade tripped on a chair and fell on his back. The gun left his hand and skidded under the bed. He rolled like a cat, coming to hands and knees as Ward reached him. Ward dived at him blindly, grappling, and the two rolled against the wall.

Ward's hands closed around Slade's throat. They tightened down, while Slade's body thrashed like that of a turkey whose head has just been severed by an axe.

Slade's face congested darkly with blood, turning slowly blue. Ward released his throat and systematically began smashing fists into the gunfighter's face. Slade's nose seemed to burst. With each blow, his head slammed against the floor.

There was a haze of fury over Ward Reeder's eyes. He lost track of time. Slade's face was splotched with blood from his streaming nose.

Dimly Reeder heard footsteps running along the hall. Hands pulled at him but he fought them off. He fought them off as long as he could but at last they yanked him away from Slade by sheer brute strength.

He was sobbing, partly with fury, partly from shortness of breath. At the door, someone said, "Why don't you let him go? Let him finish it."

And Arch Schilling's flat, hard voice, "Shut up! Come on, drag him out of there."

Ward was literally dragged across the room. He was cursing steadily with balked fury. He caught the doorjamb as they dragged him through and clung to it desperately, glaring at Arch Schilling's face. Arch said furiously, "I told you . . . damn it, I told you if you killed him you'd hang."

"I didn't kill him," Ward panted, "but I wish I had."

Arch's glance went beyond him into the room. "You didn't miss it far," he growled. "If Sam hadn't sent someone for me . . ."

A man asked, "What do you want us to do with Ward, Arch?"

"Take him down to the jail and lock him up."

Ward's grip on the doorjamb was broken and they dragged him down the hall. Arch heard him yelling all the way down the stairs, through the lobby and out into the street.

He looked across the room at Slade. The man was groaning and trying to turn over onto his stomach. His nose was still streaming blood. One of his eyes was turning puffy and discoloring.

Arch waited, watching coldly as Slade turned over and came to his hands and knees. After a while, Slade fought to his feet, staggered across the room and sat down on the bed.

He glared at Arch murderously, but Arch's old eyes didn't flinch. He said harshly, "If I was you, I'd stay in this room the rest of the day. I'd get on the morning train and get out of town."

"You can go straight to hell."

Arch said disgustedly, "I should have given Ward a little more time with you. But he's too good a man to hang for killin' the likes of you."

Slade's eyes held Arch's malevolently. "I'll kill him, sheriff. I'll kill him for what he did to me."

Arch shrugged. "Not tonight, you won't, because he's in jail." He turned and left the room without bothering to close the door. Before he reached the stairs, he heard it slam viciously.

Going down the stairs he scowled. It wouldn't be hard for Slade to taunt Ward into a gunfight after this. It wouldn't be hard at all. The only way he'd prevent it was by keeping Ward locked up.

But you couldn't keep a man locked up while his son's funeral was going on. He'd have to release Ward tomorrow.

He crossed the lobby and stepped out into the street. He wondered bleakly what would happen next. Slade was like a tormented rattlesnake right now, and there was no telling where he'd strike.

Chapter 9

Johnny Yoder dismounted in front of Barney Teplin's house. He tied his horse to the hitching post, the top of which was a cast-iron lion with a ring in its mouth.

He was worried about Ward Reeder. He knew how Ward must feel. Ward's fury might make him seek Slade out and if he did, he'd get killed too.

He shrugged lightly as he went up the walk. Arch wouldn't let that happen. Arch was as aware of the danger as he was himself.

He knocked lightly on the door. There was a vast discouragement in him as he stood there waiting for Barney to answer it. Sometimes it seemed as though the laws had been deliberately designed to protect men like Slade. They could kill with impunity, time after time. They developed a skill with a gun no other man could match. They could afford to let the other man draw first.

He heard sounds within Barney's house, and a moment later, Barney opened the door.

His eyes were red and his mouth was slack. He was squinting as though he had a monstrous headache. The light seemed to hurt his eyes. Johnny asked softly, "Hello, Barney. Can I come in?"

Barney hesitated, then stood aside. "Sure. Come on in."

Johnny went in. He noticed that the whisky bottle was no longer lying on the floor. It was sitting on a table that had been righted, and it was empty now. Otherwise, the room was unchanged, a shambles of senseless destruction.

Barney peered at Johnny, wincing once as a particularly painful throb went through his head. "Whadda ya want, Johnny?"

"Did you know Slade killed Cal Reeder?"

Shock touched Barney's face and turned it almost gray. He staggered across the room and collapsed into a chair. He put his head down into his hands and sat that way for a long, long time. At last, without raising his head, he asked, "Where is he now?"

"He took a room at the hotel. What's he going to do, Barney? Is he going to stay?"

"Hell, I don't know. He didn't say. I thought maybe . . . I thought he'd come home because he was tired of the way he was living, because he wanted to change."

"That was before he wrecked this room, wasn't it?"

Barney raised his head. "He didn't wreck this room. I did."

"And I suppose you dug the bottle out and had a drink just because you wanted one."

Barney didn't answer him. Johnny could imagine how it had been, with Slade home for the first time in more than five years. Slade had probably asked for a drink. He had probably urged Barney to drink with him and Barney, glad for any closeness between himself and his son, had accepted. One drink was all it took to start a man like Barney off. Johnny was willing to bet Slade knew that and did it deliberately — as deliberately as he had wrecked this room.

He said, "I'll help you clean this up."

Barney shook his head, wincing as he did. "Let it go. I'll do it later, myself."

Johnny said, "Arch wants you to sign a complaint. He wants an excuse to throw Slade in jail."

Barney glanced at him, fear showing in

his eyes. "Slade wouldn't go to jail. He'd kill Arch first."

"You let Arch and me worry about that. Will you sign the complaint?"

Barney shook his head. He stared at the floor. "I can't. He didn't do it. I did it myself."

Johnny said, "Barney, think! Cal isn't going to be the only one. As long as Slade's loose with that gun of his . . ."

Barney stared at Johnny warily, a growing suspicion showing in his eyes. Johnny knew instantly what he was thinking — that Johnny wanted Slade locked up for personal reasons.

Johnny said, "You're wrong, Barney. This isn't my idea. It's Arch's."

Barney didn't reply, and after a moment Johnny said, "But you're right about one thing. He and I are going to tangle if he tries to get Molly back."

A spasm of something like pain crossed Barney's face. He buried his face in his hands again. "I can't think! Oh God, I can't think straight! I need a drink."

Johnny said patiently, "That's the last thing you need. What you need is to admit what Slade is — what he's turned into since he left here five years ago. He's a killer,

Barney. He's a mad dog killer. He's so full of hate he's sick with it. He couldn't stand to see you with a decent job and a decent place to live. In less than a day he's wrecked everything you worked so hard to get."

Barney didn't bother to deny it. Johnny went on, "Do you think he's finished with you? Do you think his hate is satisfied? You know damn well it's not. Sign that complaint, Barney. Let Arch and me put Slade in jail."

Barney said bitterly, without raising his head, "And how long could you keep him there?"

"Maybe long enough to figure something out."

Barney snorted disgustedly. "A week. A week at the most. And then he'd be out again."

"A week's better than nothing at all. Maybe . . ."

Barney asked, "How did he get into a fight with Cal?"

"Cal started it," Johnny said reluctantly. "He drew first."

"Did Slade — did Slade try to stop him?"

Again Johnny nodded reluctantly. "But he didn't try hard enough. He could have turned his back. He could have just refused. I was right outside the saloon but I couldn't get through the crowd. If I'd had a couple of minutes more, I'd have had Cal. I'd have gotten to him and been able to stop it before he drew his gun."

Barney sat silently, his head down in his hands. He was still so long, Johnny thought he had gone to sleep. He got up.

But Barney was not asleep. He spoke softly, hoarsely, "I can't sign a complaint against Slade. You can see why, can't you? I let him down when he was a boy. I went on the bottle after his mother died and I'm to blame for whatever he is now. As long as there's a chance he came home to try and change . . ." He glanced up, suddenly, and Johnny was startled to see tears streaming down his cheeks. Barney's voice was almost a cry. "He's my son. He's . . . his mother's son too. I've got to give him a chance to change because I think that's why he's home."

Johnny could see Barney didn't believe what he had said. He didn't believe that Slade had come home to try and change. He believed, as Johnny did, that Slade had come home to satisfy his hatred of the town.

But he knew he'd never persuade Barney

to sign the complaint Arch wanted. He shrugged and said gently, "All right, Barney. But stay off the whisky or he won't get the chance you think he wants."

He went out, closing the door softly behind him. Standing uncertainly on the porch, he pulled out his watch and looked at it. It was three-forty-five.

He hurried to the street, mounted and whirled his horse. He headed toward the school.

He passed perhaps half a dozen children walking home. He breathed a soft sigh of relief when he saw Molly's buggy still sitting with its shafts resting on the ground. He dismounted and tied his horse.

Tommy Schilling and Tony Sanchez were staying after school, punishment, he supposed, for playing truant earlier. As he came into the classroom, Molly said, "Tommy, you and Tony can go now. You go straight home. If I hear that you've been hanging around in town . . ."

The pair got up and shuffled from the room. The door slammed behind them.

Molly looked at Johnny. Her face was pale and drawn. Fear was strong in her eyes. "Johnny, please go away. Please."

He stared at her with exasperation. "Listen

to me. You're not going back to him. Do you know what he did to Barney — to his own father?"

She shook her head numbly.

"He got Barney drunk and Barney hasn't had a drink for years. He took a shotgun like a club and deliberately wrecked the parlor of Barney's house. I won't let him near you, Molly. No matter what you say."

She turned her back on him and walked to the window. Johnny said, "He didn't come home to change. He came home because hatred for this town has been smoldering in him all these years. He came home to hurt everybody in town just as much as he possibly could."

She remained at the window, not speaking. Johnny shouted angrily, "And that includes you too. He'll hurt you all he can and then throw you away again."

When she turned to face him, her face was white, her lips compressed. She cried, "You're a fool, Johnny Yoder! Can't you get it through your stupid head that I *want* him back! Why do you think I married him? Why do you think I've waited all these years?"

Johnny said, "That won't work, Molly. So give it up."

She began to cry, softly, almost silently. She turned to face the window again. Her shoulders shook with her weeping.

Johnny crossed the room. Gently he put his hands on her shoulders. He said, "Part of loving someone is believing in them. You've got to believe in me. I'm not going to play Slade's game. Killing me is going to be a lot harder for him than killing Cal."

She turned and buried her face in his chest. He held her tightly for a long, long time, until her weeping quieted. Then he said, "I'll hitch up your buggy and take you home."

She nodded and he released her. He went to the door and out into the schoolyard. The sun was dropping toward the horizon, but it was still hot.

He untied her horse and led him to the buggy. He backed him between the shafts and hitched him up.

Molly came out of the school and crossed the yard. He helped her into the buggy, then got his own horse and tied him on behind. He'd done this every afternoon for months, until it had become routine.

He climbed into the buggy beside her and picked up the reins. He drove out of the schoolyard and down the street toward Main.

Turning into Main, he saw several men dragging a shouting Ward Reeder down the street toward the jail. As he came abreast of the hotel, Arch came out of the door and stepped off the porch.

Johnny drew the buggy to a halt. He looked at Arch questioningly.

Arch stared at him. He said grimly, "Ward just beat Slade Teplin up."

Beside Johnny, Molly gasped. Arch said, "I'm giving you two weeks off. You take Molly and go somewhere. Go a long ways off. Drive all night if you have to, but get out of Cottonwood County and get out fast."

Arch glanced up at the hotel. Then he turned and headed toward the jail. Johnny looked that way and saw Ward Reeder being forcibly dragged inside.

He slapped the back of the buggy horse with the reins. The animal trotted down the dusty street.

Johnny resisted the compulsion to look around at the windows of the hotel. He had the feeling that if he did, he would meet Slade Teplin's eyes. He could almost feel them on him, burning, searing with their intensity.

Molly sat huddled on the seat beside him,

staring straight ahead. He wondered what her reaction to Arch's suggestion was.

Whatever it was, he knew he couldn't go. He couldn't abandon Arch to handle Slade by himself. And furthermore, he knew it would do no good to run from Slade. Slade would follow. He'd find them no matter where they went.

If they ran and if Slade followed them — everything would favor Slade and all the disadvantage would be on Johnny's side. If he was with Molly any abuse of her would force him to fight no matter how much he wanted to avoid a showdown with Slade.

But if he stayed here . . . at least he had a chance. Not much of one, but at least a chance.

He frowned worriedly as the buggy horse clattered across the bridge.

Chapter 10

Slade Teplin slammed the door savagely behind the sheriff. He raised a hand and swiped at his bleeding nose.

He stood there beside the door, trembling, for a long moment. Then he drew back a foot and kicked the door with sheer frustrated fury.

He turned and crossed the room to the washstand. He bent over the basin and splashed water into his face. It stung as it touched the abrasions on his face.

He picked up the towel and mopped at his bleeding, dripping face. His whole body seemed to be trembling, from his hands down to his knees. His face worked with helpless rage. He'd kill Ward Reeder. Just as soon as the sheriff released the man from jail.

Slade was not a brawler. He was a finely tuned instrument, trained for one thing and one thing alone. He could draw and shoot his gun faster than any man alive. He could hit a four-inch target at fifty feet nine times out of ten. Not for nearly ten years had he been mauled and beaten the way Ward Reeder had beaten him.

He walked to the window and stared down into the street. He saw Arch Schilling step into sight from the hotel porch. He saw a buggy draw to a halt in front of him.

The buggy top hid the occupants, except for their knees and feet. But he knew who they were. That deputy, Yoder. And Molly, his wife.

His face twisted and his eyes narrowed murderously. He stared down at the buggy top as though he could penetrate it with the intensity of his glance.

The sheriff glanced up at the hotel, then walked on down the street. The buggy clattered after him. As it moved away downstreet he could see Molly and a moment later, the deputy. Neither looked around.

He stared after the buggy until it bounced across the railroad tracks. Then he turned, crossed the room and got down on his hands and knees beside the bed to retrieve his gun.

It lay against the wall and he had to

crawl under the bed to reach it. Doing so improved his disposition not at all. He got up again and dropped the gun into its holster at his side.

He walked back to the window and stared broodingly into the street. Everything about this stinking town held memories for him, he thought. And the memories were not pleasant ones.

Up the street from the hotel was Silverstein's Mercantile, but it had been Zachary's then. He'd worked there from five in the morning until six at night for fifty cents a day. Even now he could remember the way his muscles had ached at night. Sometimes they'd ached so bad he'd just laid in bed and wept because he couldn't go to sleep.

He muttered a savage, obscene curse. If he hated this town it was because this town had taught him hate.

He turned his head and glanced down-street at the Emporia. It was out in front of the Emporia that he'd killed his first man. He stared into the sun-washed, dusty street, and for a moment it seemed as if that day had returned. He was standing in the street, so scared his mouth was dry and his chest had turned to ice. He could hear himself — cursing — pouring out on that drifter all the bitter hatred he felt for the town, for his father and for humanity. He could feel the cold grips of the gun in his hand and could feel his hand trembling.

He'd have fired, he realized now, whether the drifter had drawn his gun or not. But the drifter *had* drawn his gun and his doing so had given the encounter the appearance of a fight.

Slade admitted to himself that the town had given him a break in acquitting him. But he did not give them credit for their motives in doing so. They had acquitted him because they were ashamed, not because they liked him. Not a single person in town had liked him. They hadn't then and they didn't now. What he did not admit was that he'd never given anyone a chance to like him. He'd been too angry to be likable. He was still angry. He had been angry all his life.

But he had come back at last. He had come back to cleanse himself of hate. He had come back to exact revenge for what the town had done to him, for what they had made of him.

He began to pace back and forth restlessly. The room was hot and his body felt like ice. His head ached savagely from the pounding Reeder had given him.

He found himself remembering other things. The taunting he had taken at school because his clothes were ragged and dirty, because his hair was shaggy and uncut, because his father was what he was. He remembered his shame whenever he found his father lying in an alley, reeking of liquor, snoring like a hog in a mud wallow.

The drifter had been the first. Until today, that drifter had been the only victim of Slade's gun here in Cottonwood Springs. But there had been other victims, in other places. Seventeen, including Cal Reeder. He sat down on the edge of the bed, finding obscure satisfaction in remembering each one of them.

From a world filled with endless weariness, shame and poverty he had worked himself into a world of awe and fear. Men looked at him nowadays with respect. They called him Mister Teplin and they did so respectfully. Some of them were ingratiating, wanting to buy him drinks, wanting to be seen in his company.

There were others, too, and without these, living would have still been hard for Slade. These were the ones who wanted to hire him to kill someone who was in their way and whom they had not the guts or skill to kill for themselves.

Slade could come into a community and kill with impunity. All he had to do was pick a quarrel with the victim and taunt him into drawing first. Then he could collect his fee and leave. It was ironic that the law protected him and others of his kind and this was a hold-over from an ancient dueling code, a code that permitted men to settle their differences for themselves as long as they adhered to certain rules.

Slade's rewards varied, of course. He had killed for as little as fifty dollars. He had received as much as a thousand. Sometimes he didn't even have to kill to collect his pay. His appearance in a particular locality occasionally was enough to make his employer's enemies capitulate.

He got up from the side of the bed and walked to the washstand again. There was a brownish stain of blood in the water. Slade stared into the mirror at his face.

His nose had stopped bleeding. So had the abrasions on his face. His lower lip was puffy, though. And one of his eyes was likely to turn black.

He'd have to show himself like this. He'd have to show the whole town what Ward

Reeder's fists had done to him. But he'd also show them something else. As soon as Reeder got out of jail, he'd show them what happened to a man who laid a hand on him.

He bent his head and again washed his face. He dampened his hair and ran a comb through it. He took off his blood-spotted shirt and got a clean one from his valise. He knotted his tie carefully and put on his coat.

He slipped his gun from its holster and checked it. He punched out the empty and re-filled the cylinder from his cartridge belt. Right now he wanted a couple of drinks. Later, he'd have supper in the hotel dining room. Then he'd get a horse at the livery barn and ride out to Molly's place. Maybe he'd spent the night out there. Hell, she was his wife, wasn't she? And besides, he needed a woman tonight.

He opened the door and stepped out into the hall. As he went down the stairs, he found himself thinking of that deputy. Yoder was smart, he realized. He was probably smart enough not to let himself he sucked into a gunfight with Slade Teplin. But there were ways of getting around him, Teplin thought. If he went out and spent the night with Molly . . . that would stir Yoder up enough to make him fight.

He permitted himself a thin smile at the thought. As he crossed the lobby, the clerk called, "Evenin', Mr. Teplin."

He turned his head and looked at the young man, who could not steadily meet his eyes. This pleased him too, the way men almost always looked away from him.

He went outside. He made a little bet with himself that no one would mention the way his face looked. He turned toward the Emporia, after first looking the street over carefully in a leisurely, deliberate way.

It was the one thing he feared — that someone who had not the courage to face him would shoot him in the back. That was a gunfighter's nightmare.

He passed the Ace-High, pacing along deliberately, and heard someone say, "There he is! There's Slade Teplin!"

He didn't turn his head. He reached the Emporia and went inside.

Almost instantly, he felt every eye on him. It was a familiar feeling and one he enjoyed. He crossed to the bar and liked, too, the way men moved aside to make a place for him.

The bartender came toward him immediately and Slade said softly, "Whisky." He stared into the backbar mirror critically as the man moved away to get a bottle and glass.

But he wasn't looking at himself. He was looking behind him. He could always tell when someone was thinking of trying him out. There were several signs that gave it away — wide eyes, the dilated pupils of those eyes, the facial pallor, and sometimes trembling hands or hands so clammy their owner continually wiped their palms against his pants.

The bartender brought his drink. The man next to Slade said, "Let me buy that drink for you, Mr. Teplin. I'm Phil Regan."

Slade turned his cold eyes on the man. He didn't protest and the man shoved some money across the bar. Regan said almost breathlessly, "This town ain't had so much excitement in years — not since King Fisher passed through."

Slade stared at him until Regan looked uneasily away. Slade picked up his drink and sipped it thoughtfully.

He felt nothing but contempt for Phil Regan's kind. And he remembered Regan, too, from years ago. Regan had once threatened to horsewhip him for following his daughter, Sarah, home from school. His mouth twisted bitterly. He remembered having a crush on Sarah because she was so pretty and so clean. But he'd never gotten closer to her than a hundred yards.

His thoughts wandered, though his ears heard the subdued talk going on around him. Most of it was about him, but he didn't listen consciously. He was thinking that he never stood in a saloon without wondering when it would happen and from what quarter it would come. That unexpected shot, with no warning. Or a hastily shouted, "Slade Teplin! Draw, damn you!" with the gun roaring before the words were decently out of the shooter's mouth.

It was true a gunfighter enjoyed a certain immunity from prosecution for his acts. But it was also true that the law afforded him less protection than it did other citizens. He was fair game and it was up to him to see that no one got a chance to shoot him in the back.

Regan said, "Have another one, Mr. Teplin. On me."

Slade turned his head and looked at him. "Did you buy that bottle, Mr. Regan?"

Regan nodded. Slade picked up the bottle. He turned it upside down and watched the contents gurgle out at Phil Regan's feet. He glanced up at Regan's face as the last of the whisky dribbled out of the bottle.

There was the briefest flash of pure fury in Regan's eyes. It faded almost instantly to be replaced by fear. Regan dropped his glance. He licked his lips. Then he turned and hurried from the saloon.

Slade shoved the bottle across the bar. "Another one, bartender. I'll pay for this one myself."

The bartender didn't reply. But he brought the bottle and set it down on the bar with a crash.

Slade said softly, "Something the matter with you, bartender?"

The man's face flushed. He would not look at Slade. He mumbled, "Matter with me? Why should there be anything the matter with me?"

Slade smiled thinly. Down the bar a big, graying man said, "Come on, Luke. We'll have our drink at the Ace-High."

Slade glanced at him, recognizing him immediately. It was John McCracken, who owned the bank. Slade said, "Just a minute, Mr. McCracken."

McCracken paused as he passed Slade on the way to the door. Slade said quietly,

"Know where your teller is?"

"Barney?"

"Yeah. Barney. He's passed out on the floor at home. Drunker than a hog on sour mash."

McCracken said evenly, "Maybe he's got that coming to him, Slade. Any father with a son like you . . ." McCracken met Slade's glance steadily, without fear, with only loathing and contempt. Then he turned and walked on out the door.

Slade's eyes were furious. He poured himself another drink and gulped it down. It had been years since anyone had looked at him that way or spoken to him that way. God damn McCracken anyway! But he'd get to McCracken before he left.

For an instant . . . for the first time since his arrival, the faintest shadow of doubt touched his mind. The trouble was, he realized, that he had grown up here. Too many people remembered him as a boy. . . .

Then the doubt was gone. He wasn't going to stay here long. When he did go . . . after he was gone . . . they'd have another memory of him in Cottonwood Springs. This town would remember him until it turned to prairie dust.

Chapter 11

Johnny Yoder drove silently as he left the town and skirted Cottonwood Creek on the way to Molly's house. Molly sat as silently beside him, staring straight ahead.

Johnny was thinking of the coming night, because he knew what was going to happen as soon as it got dark. Slade would be riding out to Molly's place. He was still Molly's husband. He had come back because he hated the town and because he wanted revenge for what he believed the town had done to him and he wouldn't miss a chance like this. He'd assert his rights as a husband, knowing Johnny would fight him, on any terms, if he did.

And he *would* fight Slade, Johnny thought. The man was sure as hell right about that. He also knew that, in Slade's kind of fight, he would have no chance. He was better than most men with his gun, but he was far from a match for Slade.

Arch had probably been right in urging him to take Molly and leave. The trouble was, Johnny had his own pride too. If he let Slade drive him away, if he let Slade make him run . . . he'd be less of a man afterward. Besides, it would do no good. Slade would follow them. Trailing a buggy would be ridiculously easy by daylight tomorrow. Then Johnny would have to face him anyway.

Molly turned her pale, scared face to look at him. "Johnny, what are we going to do?"

He covered her hand with his big, calloused one and squeezed gently. "Let me worry about that, Molly. I'll figure something out."

"But what, Johnny? What? You can't face him — you can't fight him on his terms."

"There are still almost four hours left before it gets dark. A lot can happen in four hours."

She sat in frozen silence for a long, long time. At last she said with quiet desperation, "I've been afraid he would come back for five long years, Johnny. Until I met you, I didn't dare even think of marrying again. I knew what Slade might do when he heard." She was silent for a moment and when she spoke again, her voice was an anguished cry.

"I couldn't help myself when you came along! I couldn't! I fooled myself into thinking I had been wrong about Slade — that he didn't care — that he wouldn't come back. Now I know I was wrong. And unless we run away, Slade will . . . he'll kill you, Johnny. Like he did Cal Reeder this afternoon."

Johnny said softly, "Running wouldn't help, Molly. Slade can follow a trail. He'd find us no matter where we went. We'd just be putting it off. And maybe I've got a better chance if I have it out with him right here."

"Chance?" she said bitterly. "Johnny, you have no chance! You've got to admit that and not let him goad you into a fight. I may be his wife, but he's not going to force me into anything!"

Johnny said, "Then we've got nothing to worry about."

He drew the buggy to a halt in front of her tiny house. He helped her down, then climbed back up and drove the buggy across the yard. He unhitched, led the horse to the stable and took the harness off. He led the horse to the creek and let him drink. Then he returned him to the stable and threw him several forks full of hay from a loose pile in one corner.

He returned to the house, leaving his saddle horse tied to the buggy. He went into the kitchen.

Molly had a fire going in the stove. She pulled the graniteware coffee pot forward so that it would heat. He noticed that her hands were trembling.

He crossed the room and put his arms around her. He kissed her cheek.

She turned and threw her arms around him desperately. She clung to him fiercely, as though she would never let him go.

He held her this way for a long, long time. Then her body went limp. She dropped her arms and stood listlessly, as though she had lost all hope.

Johnny said, "I've got to get back. But I'll see you again before it gets dark. He won't come out here before dark."

She nodded, avoiding his eyes.

He studied her suspiciously. He said, "You've got something going in that pretty head of yours. What is it?"

She refused to raise her glance. He took her shoulders in his hands and forced her to look at him. What he saw in her eyes was determination, quiet and fearful but implacable. He asked, "You wouldn't be think-

131

ing of shooting him yourself, would you?"

"What if I am?"

"Molly, don't be a fool! You'd go to prison for it."

"Not if I said it was self-defense."

"Who'd believe it, Molly? Everybody in town knows I've been seeing you. Everybody knows I want to marry you."

"They also know Slade. They know how violent he is."

"They know how damned careful he is too. They know he wouldn't dare hurt you. Too many people are just waiting for him to make one mistake."

He released her. He crossed the room and picked up the rifle from a corner of the room. He said, "I'll take this with me, just in case. And you stop worrying. I'll handle Slade somehow."

At the door he turned and glanced back at her. Tears of helplessness were overflowing from her eyes. He didn't want to leave but knew he must. He felt her eyes on him all the way across the yard.

He untied his horse and mounted. He smiled at her, trying to make his smile show a confidence he did not feel. Then he rode out toward town.

He felt a rising irritability as he rode. He

was beginning, already, to get sick of Slade Teplin and the problems he had raised. And while he knew feeling thus was dangerous, he still could not help himself.

It was twenty minutes of five when he halted his horse in front of the jail. He looped the reins around the rail and went inside.

After the heat of the afternoon sun outside, the office seemed cool. Arch was sitting in his swivel chair, feet on the desk, pipe in his mouth. He wore a faint frown.

Johnny asked, "Ward all right?"

"Uh-huh. But I'm scared to let him out. He wouldn't last thirty minutes if I did." He stared at Johnny irritably. "I thought I told you to keep going."

"What good would it do? Slade can follow buggy tracks. He'd catch up with us tomorrow."

"Maybe not. Maybe he wouldn't even try."

"You don't believe that. And neither do I."

There was a clatter of hoofbeats in the street and two plunging horses pulled up in front of the jail. Glancing out, Johnny saw Ward Reeder's two hired men, Les Isaacs and Willy Hogg. They tied their horses and came in.

Les was a tall, gangling man, all elbows and knees and feet. He had an unruly shock of yellow hair and a two-day growth of whiskers. Willy was of medium height and slightly overweight. He looked soft, but Johnny knew that was deceptive. No one who worked as hard as Willy did could be soft.

Les asked in a soft, southern drawl, "You know where Ward is, Arch? He left a note for us — said Cal had been killed. Is that true?"

Arch nodded. He gestured with his head toward the jail cells at the rear. "He's out there in a cell. Go talk to him if you want."

Les stared puzzledly at him, then at Johnny. With a faint shrug he said, "Come on, Willy."

The two crossed the office and opened the door leading to the cells. Johnny heard them say hello to Ward. Then the door closed and after that he could only hear the murmur of voices behind it.

He asked, "Think he'll put them up to something, Arch?"

"Mebbe. I know he'll try. I'll talk to them before they leave." Arch studied Johnny carefully. "What I want to know is what *you* are going to do. Suppose Slade goes out to

Molly's place tonight?"

"I'll stop him. One way or another, I'll stop him before he gets there."

"He has a right . . ."

"Right hell! He's got no rights at all. He doesn't give a damn about her, or he wouldn't have stayed away from her this long. The only reason he'd go out there would be to start something. With me. He can't stand for this town to know Molly prefers me to him."

"Maybe I ought to just order him to leave town."

"You can't make it stick."

"I can try."

"There's no train out until nine-thirty tomorrow morning. By then, it'll probably be too late."

Les and Willy came out of the door leading to the cells. Arch said, "I don't know what Ward said to you two, but take my advice and don't do anything stupid. You work for Ward, but it ain't part of your job to get killed for him."

Les gave him a slow grin. "Don't worry, Arch. We ain't about to choose Slade, if that's what you're driving at."

"Fine. Cal's body is across the street at Jim Hawkins' place, if you want to see it."

"That's what Ward said. I reckon we'll just mosey over there and see Cal. You're gonna let Ward out in time for the funeral in the mornin', ain't you?"

Arch nodded.

Les made a slow, deliberate smile. "So long, Arch."

Arch grunted sourly. Les and Willy went out and started across the street. Arch said, "Ward's put them two up to something, sure as hell. You watch, Johnny. When they come out of Hawkins' store, follow 'em. Keep an eye on 'em for a while."

Johnny nodded. Arch got up ponderously and went back to talk to Ward. Johnny doubted if he'd get anything out of Ward Reeder, but it wouldn't hurt to try. Arch closed the door and again Johnny heard the murmur of voices behind it.

Les and Willy disappeared into the furniture store. A buckboard passed the jail, heading out of town. A few minutes later, two men on saddle horses entered town and passed, heading toward the hotel. Johnny didn't recognize them. From the looks of them, they were just drifting through.

Les and Willy emerged across the street. They came across to the jail, untied their horses and mounted. They rode up the street and stopped in front of the Emporia where they talked for a minute. Then Willy rode on up the street and turned the corner. Les dismounted, tied his horse and went into the Emporia.

Johnny grabbed his hat and went outside. There were long shadows now in the street. The air was hot and still. Johnny smelled woodsmoke in it, and the smell of frying meat.

It was a little after five. He hurried along the street, but he didn't believe Les would be fool enough to start anything with Slade. Certainly not all by himself. Still, rangeland loyalties were strong, and he could not be sure.

He went into the Emporia and paused for an instant just inside the doors. Les was at the near end of the bar. Farther along, Johnny saw Slade Teplin, a bottle and glass in front of him. There was a strong odor of whisky in the place, as though some had been spilled.

Slade's head turned as he came in. His face was cold and expressionless. One of his eyes was turning black and his mouth was puffy. There were several noticeable abrasions on his face. His eyes, staring so steadily at Johnny, were malevolent.

Les turned his head and grinned at Johnny as he approached. "Arch tell you to check up on me?"

Johnny returned his grin, liking Les. He nodded. "He just wants to be sure you don't dig your grave with that big mouth of yours."

"Don't worry. I ain't that stupid."

Sam Riordan called, "What'll you two have?"

Les yelled, "Couple of beers, Sam!" He glanced at Johnny. "That all right with you?"

Johnny nodded. Sam brought two thick mugs of beer and Les slid a dime across the bar. Johnny sipped the beer. He could feel Slade's eyes on him. It made him both angry and nervous, wondering what the man was thinking, what he intended to do. Les murmured softly, "He's sure watching you, Johnny. He sure as hell is."

Johnny shrugged, but he did not glance toward Slade. Suddenly, Les gulped his beer. He said hastily, "See you, Johnny," and ducked away from the bar, heading toward the door.

Arch needn't have worried about Les taking Slade on, Johnny thought. He acted like he was scared to death.

The incongruity of it struck him suddenly. Les wasn't a scary man. And Johnny was willing to bet he wasn't really scared of Slade. Not enough to run just because the man approached.

He turned his head. Slade came up beside him, carrying his bottle and glass. He put the glass down and dumped some whisky into it. He said, without looking at Johnny, "I want to talk to you."

Johnny's body was suddenly as tight-drawn as a fiddlestring. His heart felt as though it was trying to beat a hole in his chest. He waited a moment before he answered, and when he did his voice was steady and in-different. "All right," he said, "talk away."

Chapter 12

Slade turned his head. He looked straight into Johnny's eyes and said, "You're a dirty, back-alley, wife-stealing son-of-a-bitch."

So unexpectedly did the words come, and in such an unemotional tone of voice, that for an instant Johnny was stunned, almost unbelieving. Words like that should be spoken in fury, not the way Slade had spoken them.

But an instant later he understood. There was no passion in Slade. He didn't love his wife, didn't even want her, really. He was just looking for a fight.

The instant comprehension struck him, Johnny felt his wild, sudden anger begin to fade. He said in an equally unemotional voice, "And you're a murdering, mad-dog killer that wouldn't know a fair fight if it hit you in the face."

Slade stepped away from the bar. Johnny

knew what was coming. Slade would back slowly away until ten or fifteen feet separated them. Then he'd begin cursing Johnny and if that didn't work, he'd bring Molly into it, defiling her with his words until Johnny could stand no more.

Johnny's hand went out suddenly. He grabbed Slade by his shirt-front and yanked him close. Simultaneously his knee came up, catching Slade in the crotch.

Slade's gun was already in his hand. Johnny batted his hand as the gun came up, deflecting the muzzle, deflecting the bullet that roared out on a searing lance of flame and smoke.

Releasing Slade's shirt front with his right hand, he seized the man's wrist with it. With his left hand he twisted Slade's gun away and flung it savagely across the room.

Slade was sick. His face was almost green with the pain of Johnny's knee. Johnny knew he'd never get another chance like this. Slade was disarmed and sick. He'd created a disturbance and for that Johnny could throw him into jail.

Deftly he seized Slade's left arm, twisted it until it was behind the gunman's back. He raised it until Slade winced with pain. He said with soft breathlessness, "All right, gunfighter, you can cool off tonight in jail."

He pushed Slade, unresisting, toward the door. He heard the collective sigh that seemed to come simultaneously from every man in the room. He reached the door as Les Isaacs settled in his saddle in the street and realized with a shock that everything that had taken place had happened in the time Les had needed to walk out of the Emporia, untie and mount his horse.

Slade had found his voice and was now cursing Johnny in words that were unbelievably obscene. Johnny said harshly, "Shut up, or by God we'll leave a trail of your teeth all the way from here to the jail."

Slade's cursing continued, unabated. He finished with Johnny and started cursing Molly. Johnny released his arm and gave him a push. Slade turned in time to catch Johnny's clenched fist squarely in the mouth. He staggered back, with Johnny following murderously.

Chopping rights and lefts smashed into Slade's face. He retreated, staggering, down the street toward the jail. Back in front of the Emporia a man yelled, "Kill him, Johnny! Kill the son-of-a-bitch!"

Johnny suddenly dropped his hands. He

said savagely, "Git! Get on down to the jail before I do kill you!"

Slade glared at him murderously for a moment, then turned and shuffled toward the jail. Following him, Johnny wondered for the first time whether what he'd done was right. He hadn't really had much choice. It had been this or facing Slade on Slade's own terms.

He saw Arch come out of the jail and glance toward him. Arch stood there staring unbelievingly, but as Slade drew close, a grin spread slowly across Arch's face. He held the door for Slade with mock ceremony and Slade went in, scowling fiercely. Johnny followed.

Inside the office, Slade made a rush for the gunrack. He seized one of the shotguns and whirled —

Johnny drew his gun and fired. His bullet tore into the floor a couple of inches from Slade's foot. Slade dropped the shotgun as though it was too hot to hold.

Johnny stood there glaring at him challengingly, waiting. Slade turned and shuffled toward the door leading to the cells. He opened it and meekly went into one of the cells. Johnny slammed the barred door and turned the key in the lock. He withdrew the key.

Ward Reeder got up and came to the bars of his cell, grasping them with both his hands. He didn't speak, but his knuckles were white. He glowered at Slade for a long time before he said between clenched teeth, "You ain't turnin' out to be such a big man after all, are you, killer?"

Slade spat toward him viciously, then sat down on the bunk. Johnny went back to the office and closed the door.

Arch asked, "What happened?"

"He started cussin' me out in the saloon. He began to back away so he could start a gunfight but I grabbed him and roughed him up before he could. I guess we could charge him with creating a disturbance, couldn't we?"

"Sure. We can hold him until morning that way. Unless we decide to file a formal charge. If we do, we might make it last a week."

"Let's see what happens between now and tomorrow. Somehow or other, I don't think Slade is going to be in jail very long."

"What the hell are you talking about?"

"The town's beginning to get mad. Someone hollered at me to kill the son-of-a-bitch a while ago."

Arch frowned, but he didn't speak. Johnny rolled a cigarette with fingers that trembled slightly. He licked it and stuck it into his mouth. He lighted it, then sank down on the office cot.

The showdown had been postponed at least, he thought. Molly would be safe tonight. He got up suddenly. "I'd like to ride out to Molly's place and tell her Slade's in jail. She's probably worried sick."

"Sure, go ahead."

Johnny went out, untied his horse and mounted. He whirled the horse and galloped out of town, only slowing for the plank bridge that spanned the creek.

He held the horse to a steady lope all the way to Molly's place. He saw her come out and stand, her hand upraised to shield her eyes from the late afternoon sun. He pounded into the yard and swung, grinning, from his horse. "Slade's in jail. You can quit worrying, at least for tonight."

She stood there, frozen, staring at him almost uncomprehendingly. Then she lowered her hand and ran toward him.

He caught her in his arms. She was laughing and crying at the same time. He squeezed her, hard, then held her away, grinning.

"How did that happen, Johnny? What did he do?"

He told her swiftly all that had happened. As he did, a cloud seemed to cross her face. "How long can you keep him in jail?"

"Overnight."

"Then come out for supper, Johnny. I'll fix something special."

He nodded, studying her face, his own expression sober. Her thoughts were the same as his own in one respect, he realized. She knew, as he did, that he had only postponed the inevitable. And yet, he had given himself a respite by throwing Slade in jail. He had given her a respite too.

He said, "I'll go and stay at the jail until Arch has had supper. Then I'll come back."

She nodded. "I'll have it ready about seven."

He bent his head and kissed her thoroughly. He felt his blood begin to pound crazily. If she didn't marry him soon . . .

Her face was flushed as he released her and swung to the back of his horse. She met his glance, then glanced away.

He knew what was in Molly's mind, and suddenly he loved her more than he ever had before. She was going to let him stay out here with her tonight. She was afraid that tomorrow . . . that there might not be another night for them. Tonight was going to have to take the place of the lifetime together that they had planned.

The realization stirred wild excitement in him, and made him temporarily forget Slade Teplin altogether. But he did not forget him long. The town came into sight and he crossed the plank bridge below the railroad tracks. Suddenly Slade became an insoluble problem once more.

He dismounted in front of the jail and went inside. Slade and Ward Reeder were yelling at each other behind the closed door leading to the cells. He glanced at Arch. "How long has this been going on?"

"Ever since you left."

"Molly asked me for supper, Arch. Why don't you go ahead and eat? She said it wouldn't be ready until about seven."

Arch noded. Johnny opened his mouth to ask Arch if he could have the rest of the evening off but he closed it without saying anything. He was suddenly embarrassed, knowing Arch would realize why he asked, would know exactly what was in the wind.

This was, actually, his night off anyway. He'd spent last night here at the jail. Last night had been his night to put the town to bed.

Arch took his hat off the coat-tree and went out. The shouting in the cells had stopped. Probably both Slade and Ward were out of breath, Johnny thought.

He sat down in Arch's swivel chair, frowning to himself. He couldn't rid himself of a strange uneasiness, a feeling that something was going to happen. He scoffed at the feeling. He didn't see what could happen now. Ward was in jail and so was Slade.

He got up and went to the window. The sun was low on the horizon and the whole street was shady from the buildings on the west side of Main, from the cottonwood trees beyond. A light breeze had sprung up and little puffs of cotton from the trees drifted lazily across the street.

Activity in the street was almost normal now. He wondered how Barney was. He wondered if Barney would be able to throw off the setback he'd had this morning. He knew that once a reformed drunk had a drink, he was usually back on the stuff again. He hoped it wouldn't be true of Barney. Barney had had enough trouble as it was.

He saw the two strangers he'd noticed earlier come out of the Emporia and stand talking on the walk in front of it. Both of them were looking at the jail. After several moments they untied their horses and mounted. They rode down the street past the jail not looking at it until they drew abreast. Their stares were steady and appraising, but when they saw Johnny they looked away. They continued down the street to Regan's livery and turned in.

Johnny frowned. They were going to stay the night, he thought, and wondered why.

Disgustedly he turned away from the window. He was getting to be a regular old woman. Sure they'd stared at the jail. They'd been told Slade Teplin was here, and they were curious. Just like everybody else in town.

And why the hell shouldn't they stay the night if they wanted to? Drifters came through all the time, especially in the spring and fall, looking for work on the ranches that surrounded Cottonwood Springs for fifty miles in all directions.

These two didn't seem any different from the others that had come and gone over the past month or so. They certainly didn't look like Slade Teplin's kind, even though they did wear guns.

He returned to the window in time to see

the pair come from Regan's and walk back up the street. They walked on the far side, and this time they only glanced disinterestedly at the jail. He watched them until they turned in at the hotel.

He turned away from the window, surprised at his own nervousness. He crossed the office, opened the door leading to the cells and glanced inside. Ward Reeder was sitting on his cot and so was Slade. Both of them looked at him, Ward resentfully, Slade with quiet virulence. Neither spoke.

For some reason, Johnny glanced at both cell windows, and wondered why he did. He closed the door and began to pace restlessly back and forth.

Hell, he was being stupid and ridiculous. Both cell windows were securely barred. The bars were set in stone. They'd have to be sawed through before either prisoner could escape.

He rolled another cigarette and forced himself to stand still while he smoked it. But he couldn't quiet his uneasiness. He couldn't calm his jumping nerves no matter how he tried.

Chapter 13

It was still not quite six o'clock. Johnny saw Arch go into the hotel. A few moments later he saw John McCracken come out of the bank. McCracken locked the door and strode away toward home.

Tonight, the street seemed ordinary, neither busier nor less busy than usual. With Slade Teplin in jail, most of the curiosity seekers had disappeared.

Johnny turned away from the window, frowning faintly to himself. He couldn't entirely get rid of his uneasiness. Jailing Slade had been too easy, he supposed, to seem believable.

He crossed the room and picked up the shotgun Slade had dropped. He returned it to the rack. He headed for Arch's swivel chair, catching movement out of the corner of his eye as he did.

Two riders were passing the jail, coming

from the north end of town. He stared at them, his frown deepening.

Two more drifters, looking much like the first two had. And suddenly Johnny didn't believe in the coincidence of two pairs of them arriving by chance today.

He walked to the window and studied them carefully. One was about forty, he guessed, and the other was probably around twenty-five. Both were dressed in range clothes, dusty from the trail. Their shirts were rimmed with sweat at the armpits and down the back, its salt showing white against the dark blue of the shirts. Both had several days' growth of whiskers on their faces.

They passed, dismounted before the Emporia and disappeared inside.

Johnny got up quietly and crossed to the door at the rear of the office. He flung it open.

Slade was standing at the window of his cell, looking out. Ward Reeder was sitting on the edge of his bunk, staring disconsolately at the floor at his feet.

Johnny frowned, thinking of the two drifters that had just now passed and of the other two.

All four, he realized, were so ordinary, so

average he would have difficulty in describing them. What the hell was he worrying about?

He closed the door, returned to the window and stared into the street. It was deserted now. Everyone had gone home for supper, or had gone into the hotel to eat.

Suddenly, from the direction of the deserted livery stable across from Regan's he heard a volley of shots. He burst through the door and stopped, listening, on the walk.

Another volley of shots racketed down there. Johnny began to run toward the sounds.

Halfway to the place he stopped and glanced back uneasily at the jail. He shouldn't leave with Slade locked up. . . .

He hesitated there in the middle of the street. Men were running out of the hotel and out of both saloons. They made an uncertain cluster in the street, their faces white and all turned this way.

Johnny thought he heard a shout back at the jail. He whirled and began to run.

He burst in through the open door, crossed the office and yanked open the door leading to the cells. He stopped instantly.

Ward Reeder had gone. The bars at his window had been literally torn out, as though by a giant hand.

Slade Teplin yelled, "You goddam stupid fool! Where were you? They hitched a team to those bars and just yanked 'em out. They . . ."

Johnny's gun was in his hand. He ran back, plunged through the door and rounded the corner at full speed. The team was still standing just below the window of the cell Reeder had occupied. But Ward was gone and so was the man who had brought the team.

Johnny cursed softly, disgustedly to himself. They'd had to draw him away from the jail so he wouldn't hear Slade's shouts or the noise of the bars breaking loose. One of Reeder's men had fired a couple of volleys over behind the deserted livery barn. As soon as Johnny ran that way, the other had hooked a chain to the bars. The whole thing hadn't taken more than two or three minutes at most.

He returned to the front of the jail. Arch was coming down the street, his napkin still in his hand. Johnny said angrily, "They took me in like a damn schoolboy. A few shots over there to draw me away from the jail. And while I was gone, one of 'em hitched that team to the bars and yanked 'em out."

"And now Ward's loose."

"I'm sorry, Arch."

"For what? I'd have done exactly what you did. We're both on edge. Besides, I'd have turned Ward loose tomorrow anyway." He eyed Johnny a moment as though trying to evaluate his frame of mind. Then he said, "My supper's getting cold," turned and walked back toward the hotel.

Johnny went into the jail. He felt foolish for allowing Ward to escape. But he knew why Ward had escaped and what he would try to do. He'd kill Slade if he could, in any way he could, even by shooting him through the bars of his cell.

He paced back and forth, scowling to himself, puzzled at his growing uneasiness. It was as though he sensed something that was not readily apparent yet.

Slade was yelling for him, so he opened the door and looked through at the man. Slade said, "Do something, damn you. I'm a sitting duck in here. Reeder will be along any minute and shoot me through the window. That's why he had 'em break him out."

Johnny stared at him bleakly. "What would you suggest I do? Turn you loose so you can kill Reeder before he gets to you?"

"I don't care what you do."

Johnny shrugged. "Maybe you shouldn't have come back. Maybe I'd be doing the town a favor if I let Reeder kill you."

He slammed the door angrily. Supper with Molly was out of the question now. So was taking the night off. He'd have to stay here all night.

He went outside into the street. He made a circle of the jail.

It stood by itself, surrounded by weed-grown vacant lots. The nearest building was twenty-five feet away. He wondered how and when Reeder would strike.

He returned to the front of the jail. It was ironic that he should be trying to keep Slade Teplin alive when more than anything else in the world, he wanted him dead.

Arch was coming toward him from the direction of the hotel. He was carrying a tray. Johnny held the door for him and Arch went inside. Johnny opened the cell door and Arch took the tray in to Slade. He came back out and Johnny re-locked the door. Arch said, "Go ahead and eat. I'll bring a chair back here. If Ward shows up at one of those windows he's going to get his head blown off."

"I can eat in town. I don't have to go out

to Molly's place."

"Go ahead. Ward ain't a fool. And he knows we ain't fools."

Slade glanced up from his food. "Eat a hearty meal, deputy. It's the last of my wife's cookin' *you'll* ever eat."

Johnny glanced at him disgustedly. He wondered if he should tell Arch about the drifters. He decided not to say anything, for now at least. Chances were he was worrying unnecessarily. He guessed it had been just too easy, getting Slade in jail. He hadn't believed it would be that simple and he was worrying now to compensate.

Ward Reeder constituted no real threat. He wasn't going to fight either Johnny or Arch in order to kill Slade. He'd try getting to Slade, of course, but if they remained on guard . . .

And the four drifters were probably exactly what they seemed to be. He went outside and untied his horse. He mounted and rode around to the side of the jail. He picked up the team's halter ropes and led them toward Regan's Livery Barn.

Regan was sitting on a bench out front. Johnny asked, "These yours?"

Regan nodded, got up and took the halter ropes from Johnny's hand. "I didn't know —

I didn't know what Ward was goin' to use 'em for."

"You're a liar, Phil. You knew damn well what he wanted 'em for." He stared coldly down at the man. "I wonder if Ward knows who it was that egged Cal on today."

Phil's face lost color. "I didn't . . . Ward wouldn't . . ."

"Don't count on it. If I were you, I'd stay out of sight tonight."

Phil looked physically sick. Johnny left him and rode past the railroad station.

He was thinking that Slade had been in Cottonwood Springs less than one whole day. He was thinking, too, that the day wasn't over yet.

As he clattered over the bridge, he thought of Barney, and wondered how he was. Then he kicked his horse into a lope and thundered toward Molly's place.

The sun was going down. It dipped its rim below the butte west of town, flaming pure gold and throwing visible golden rays upward into the sky. Johnny watched it sink. By the time he reached Molly's house it was beneath the horizon and the clouds above were flaming with its afterglow.

Molly came to the door and watched him approach. She had changed her dress. Her hair caught the gold color from the clouds.

Johnny dismounted. He grinned. "You're the prettiest thing I've seen today."

Her skin, already flushed from the stove inside, flushed even darker now. Johnny said, "I was going to clean up, but I didn't have time. Ward's two men broke him out of jail by hitching a team to the window bars."

Her face clouded and Johnny nodded unwillingly. "I'll have to eat and run. Arch and I will both have to stick around tonight."

"Why don't you just let Ward . . .?" She didn't finish but Johnny knew what she had been going to say. She said, "I didn't mean that, I guess. I don't know."

He took her in his arms and kissed her on the mouth. The kiss, which he meant to have been light, grew long and when Johnny let her go he was all stirred up. He said, "Damn Ward anyway."

She smiled, but it was a wan smile that soon faded from her face. She said, "Come in, Johnny, and wash. I'll have it ready right away."

He went in, got some hot water from a teakettle on the stove and poured it into the washpan. He washed and dried his face and hands. He sat down at the table and watched her move around the kitchen.

But his thoughts were back in town. Several things puzzled him.

Slade's return was one of them. Plainly Slade hated the town bitterly and wanted to hurt it as much as he could. His action in getting his father drunk and then wrecking things at Barney's house gave substance to that theory. Cal had been an accident, Johnny supposed. Slade couldn't have planned or anticipated Cal's challenge earlier today.

Next, he had tried to pick a fight with Johnny himself. If he'd succeeded, he would have hurt Molly by killing Johnny off. Thus, he would have hurt the two closest to him as much as they could be hurt.

But what about the rest of the town? How did he plan to go about hurting all the rest of the people he hated here? How could one man hurt a whole town anyway? How could Slade ruin Cottonwood Springs the way he had ruined Barney, the way he would have ruined Molly if he'd succeeded in killing Johnny a while ago?

That was what puzzled him, because he didn't know. A man could burn a town, he supposed, but it wouldn't be easy to do. Cottonwood Springs was a good-sized place.

There were close to four hundred people here.

And there were the four drifters. Where did they fit in? Or didn't they fit in at all?

Molly began to put food on the table. Fried chicken and cream gravy. Mashed potatoes, and a dish of early garden vegetables. He could smell an apple pie as she took it out and put it aside to cool.

He put thought of the town, of Slade and Ward, of the four strangers out of his mind. He smiled at Molly, across the table from him.

But a core of uneasiness lingered in his mind, and he unconsciously ate faster than was necessary.

Chapter 14

When Johnny left, Arch picked up a straight-backed chair and carried it through the door leading to the cells. He set it down next to the wall, then returned to the office for his pipe.

Returning, he sat down in the chair and tilted it comfortably against the wall. He glanced at Ward's window, and at Slade's, absently making sure he had a clear shot from here at both of them. Then he began to pack his pipe.

His movements were slow and deliberate. Slade glared at him. He finished packing the pipe and lighted it carefully. A cloud of smoke lifted into the upper half of the room.

Arch was thinking that what he'd told Johnny wasn't strictly accurate — not in its implications at least. True, Ward Reeder wasn't a fool. And he knew neither Arch nor Johnny was. But that didn't mean he wasn't going to try getting Slade, and Arch had implied it did.

Ward would come. Maybe he wasn't fool enough to try killing Slade through one of the jail windows but he'd figure something out.

Slade paced nervously back and forth. He kept glancing at the windows, one after the other. Once he said irritably, "Goddamn it, do we have to just sit here and wait?"

"What's the matter, you scared? Maybe if you get good and scared you'll know how all the men you've killed felt just before they died."

"They all had an even break."

"Oh sure. Like the one out in front of the Emporia years ago. The first one, in case you've forgotten him. You had your gun in your hand and he had to draw. You call that an even break?"

"That was different. That was the first one and I was just a kid."

Arch said conversationally, "I'm curious about something. What do you do when you get into an argument with someone you know is just as good as you, or maybe better?"

"We don't —" Slade stopped suddenly.

Arch smiled lazily. "Go ahead. Finish. You don't shoot it out with men like that, do you? Seems to me I can't ever remember two real fast gunmen shootin' it out with each other. Maybe they don't like the odds of taking on someone just as good as they are."

Slade was silent, frowning, obviously trying to recall one example of a gunfighter shooting it out with another of his kind.

Arch watched him speculatively for a long time. Slade's scowl deepened. Arch said finally, "So that makes it murder, doesn't it? It's just like a rigged poker game where you know you're going to win because you've stacked the cards."

"I always let the other guy draw first."

"Sure. Sure you do. You can afford to. Besides, it's smart. It gives you immunity from prosecution. But you know, every time who it is that's going to die. Like with Cal Reeder earlier today." An expression of disgust crossed Arch's hard old face. "Hell, I'd ought to let Ward Reeder have you. And I would if it wasn't for the fact that I'd have to arrest him for it."

"Watch the windows, old man, and stop shooting off your mouth."

"Yeah. Maybe I should at that. I wouldn't

164

want anything to happen to you. You ain't through with us here in Cottonwood Springs yet. You've got your pa to drinking again and you've wrecked his place, but you haven't finished with Molly, have you? Or with Johnny Yoder for wanting to marry her. Who else did you come back to get, Slade?"

He stared steadily at Slade. Slade's eyes were murderous but he didn't reply.

Arch persisted, "Who? What's the matter, can't you talk?"

"Maybe you, old blabbermouth. Maybe you."

"I suppose you hate me because you had to carry supplies out of the store for me when you were a boy."

"Why not? There you'd sit, like you thought you was God, up on your wagon seat while I sweated gettin' your goddamn stuff loaded up. You're no different from the rest of the bastards in this town."

Arch peered at him. Slade's eyes were alive with hate. His face was twisted with it. Arch said mildly, "You think you're hurting us. But you're the one that's sufferin'. I wouldn't be you for all the money in the world."

Slade whirled and strode to the window.

With his back to Arch, he stared angrily outside.

The sun was down, now, and cool shadow had crept across the town. A few high clouds, watching the sun's rays and reflecting it, threw a warm, red-gold light upon the town. It would be a hot summer, Arch thought. Probably a dry one too.

For some reason he did not himself understand, he began to think of his own early years. He'd come up from Texas with a trail herd immediately after the war. He'd liked it here and so had stayed. He'd taken up a quarter section a dozen miles north of town and, over the years, had managed to acquire, by purchase, forty or fifty more from settlers who had thought they could raise farm crops on this land. The farm crops all dried up and the buffalo grass took over once again.

Those had been good years. The juices of youth had been strong in him. He wished, though, that he'd been able to have a son. But he'd had his wife; he'd had Faith, and she had been all any man could ask. Once, he remembered, he'd even considered taking Slade to raise. But he hadn't, and right now he couldn't remember what it had been that had made him decide against doing it.

Johnny Yoder was more like the son he would have wanted, he mused. And a sudden realization struck him. He thought of Johnny almost as if Johnny had been his son. He worried every time Johnny went out after someone and it wasn't the professional worry of a sheriff for his deputy.

He chuckled deep in his throat at his own blindness. He was an old fool, he guessed. He was a damned old fool.

And yet, he told himself, he hadn't tried to spare Johnny from any of the hazards of the job. He had only worried.

He heard the street door open, pushed his chair away from the wall and stood up. He drew his gun and with it in his hand, opened the door leading to the office. He went through it, closing it behind him.

Les Isaacs and Willy Hogg were standing by the outside door. Both looked a little scared, but there was something determined about them too. Arch asked, "What do you two want?"

He had an uneasy feeling, suddenly, and knew he had to get rid of this pair quickly so that he could return to the cells and guard Slade.

Neither of the two answered him immediately and he barked, "Damn it, what do you want?"

They split, one going to the right, the other to the left. They moved casually, making it seem as though one was heading for the office couch, the other for a chair.

Arch took a backward step. Suddenly both Les and Willy had guns in their hands. Les's voice was sharper than Arch had ever heard it be. "Stick it in the holster, Arch, and sit down someplace."

Arch experienced a sudden feeling of relief, one he was ashamed of instantly. He would have a perfect alibi. Soon he'd hear a shot out back, or two or three, and after waiting a couple of minutes Les and Willy would go. He'd go back to the cells and Slade Teplin would be dead.

Johnny would be safe from Teplin's deadly gun. He'd be free to marry Molly. Barney would quit the liquor again and the town would go on as it had before. All Arch Schilling had to do was let Les and Willy hold him here. For two or three minutes at most.

No one would blame him, he thought. In fact everyone would probably be relieved.

Everyone except Ward, he thought suddenly. Ward would be the one who paid. Ward would go to trial and while no jury here would hang him, he'd at least spend a good long time in prison.

He still had his gun in his hand. He lowered it but he did not holster it. He said, "I'm going to turn my back and go through that door. I don't figure either one of you has got the stomach to shoot me in the back. But if you do, just go ahead."

Les said sharply, "Arch, goddamn it . . .!"

Arch looked at him. Les said, "He's a dirty, stinking killer, Arch! Why the hell are you so set on protecting him?"

"Slade?" Arch looked at Les in amazement. "I ain't protecting Slade. I'm thinkin' about Ward right now. Ward will get ten years for this at the very least."

He turned his back deliberately, careful to make no sudden movements that might be misconstrued. His back, at one spot in the center of it, ached suddenly. He reached out a hand for the doorknob.

Les barked, "Arch, damn you, I'll shoot!"

Arch grasped the knob. He opened the door and stepped on through.

He glanced first at Slade's window, then at the other from which the bars had been torn earlier. Then he leaned back against the door.

He felt weak. His knees trembled and he was sweating heavily. His chest felt as though there was a cake of ice in it.

He said, "Slade, get over under the window and lie down against the wall."

Slade looked at him, then suddenly dived for the window. He flopped on the floor and rolled against the wall.

Arch smiled grimly. Slade was no different from others of his kind. He could kill with icy calm as long as he knew what the outcome was going to be. But let him face death unarmed and that icy calm evaporated like dew before the rays of the morning sun.

Arch kept switching his glance back and forth, from one window to the other. Chances were, he thought, that Ward would appear at the window of what had formerly been his cell. There would be no bars there. And it commanded a good view of Slade's cell.

Arch yelled, "Ward! Don't do it because I'm waiting for you!"

There was only silence outside. Arch glanced at Slade and said contemptuously, "How does it feel, killer?"

Slade growled, "If I had a gun . . ."

"But you don't. And neither did Cal, really. He'd just as well have grabbed his tobacco for all the good it did him."

Slade didn't reply. Arch said, "I'm going

to turn you loose tomorrow morning, Slade. I'm going to escort you down to the railroad station and put you on the train — without your gun. If you come back, I'm warning you, it's open season. I'll shoot you on sight and so will my deputy."

"You can't . . . I haven't broken any of your goddamn laws."

"Get an injunction then. But until you do, stay out of Cottonwood Springs."

He heard a movement in the weeds outside the window of the cell Ward Reeder had occupied. He yelled, "Ward! Don't!"

He saw Reeder's face at the window, saw the blue barrel of Ward's gun. He fired instantly, not at Ward but at the wall beside Ward's face. The bullet rang against the stone wall like a blacksmith's hammer against an anvil. Almost instantaneously it rang again, against one of the bars on the other side of the room.

Ward swung his glance from Slade to Arch. His gun swung too. Arch yelled, "Ward! Damn it . . .!"

The gun belched flame and smoke. Something hit Arch in the chest, driving him back like the angry kick of a mule. He slammed into the chair he had just left, overturned it and fell on top of it.

Ward Reeder's face disappeared. Arch felt a numbness in his chest. He brought up a hand and felt the warmth and stickiness of blood.

He'd been shot before, but never this bad, he realized. And to get it defending a son-of-a-bitch like Slade. . . .

He tried to get up, but he could not. Still holding his gun, he crawled toward the door.

He'd closed it a few moments before, he remembered now. Somehow he had to reach high enough to turn the knob. . . .

He pulled himself as close to the door as he could. His head was reeling and clouds were forming before his eyes.

Straining, grunting softly with exertion. he reached up and turned the knob. He fell back down and moved aside enough to pull the door open. Laboriously, he crawled on through.

He crawled, inch by inch toward the outside door. Pain came now to his chest, pain worse than anything he had ever known before.

He supposed that this was it, for him. He was going to die. Damn few men made it with a bullet in the chest.

But he hung on angrily, waiting for someone to come. He couldn't give up now. Not while Slade Teplin was alive. Not until he knew for sure that Johnny Yoder was safe from him.

Chapter 15

Johnny reached the outskirts of town in the last, cool light of dusk. He had not been gone very long, he realized. He had practically bolted his food.

He could see the length of Main and the crowd spread out in front of the Ace-High and the Emporia. He muttered, "Good God, what now?"

The crowd was static, silent. It was a fearful crowd, he thought, and all faces were turned in his direction.

As he went past Regan's livery, Phil Regan called, "There were some shots in the jail a few minutes ago, Johnny. I don't know . . ."

Johnny didn't hear the last few words. He touched heels to his horse's sides, forcing him to gallop, and swung to the ground in front of the jail.

The horse stopped and stood, reins dragging on the ground, while Johnny crossed the walk at a run.

Gun in hand, he burst in through the door. The first thing he saw was Arch Schilling, lying on the floor, and the second was the blood, drenching Arch's shirt-front and pooling beneath his chest.

He ran to the rear door and flung it open. He plunged through, gun ready, hammer back.

Slade was lying on the floor against the wall staring at the window from which the bars had been yanked earlier. Johnny whirled, holstering his gun. He returned to the office, crossed to Arch and knelt at his side.

His throat felt closed and tight and it was hard for him to breath. He said, "Arch . . ."

Arch groaned slightly and stirred, but he did not open his eyes.

Johnny got up, crossed to the open front door and stepped outside. He stared toward the crowd up in front of the town's two saloons and roared, "Get Doc Allen, someone, and get him fast! It's Arch!"

He waited until he saw one man run toward Doc's office, another toward his house. Then he went back inside.

He crossed to the door leading to the rear and removed the hinge pins from it. He carried it to Arch and laid it down beside him. Arch would have to be moved, either to Doc's house or to his office, and the safest way to move a badly wounded man was on a door.

Now he paced back and forth helplessly. He had no experience with serious wounds and he didn't know what to do. He kept going to the front door and looking out and finally, as the last gray light of dusk faded from the sky, he saw Doc running toward him, carrying his bag, paced by one of the men who had gone to fetch him earlier.

He hurriedly lighted both lamps and set them on a table so that their light would shine on Arch. Doc came in and the other man followed, to stop and stand beside the door, eyes wide, face white. Doc knelt beside Arch and cut away his shirt-front to expose the wound. He studied it for a moment or two.

Doc was a short man, thick-set and growing heavier in his advancing years. His face was incredibly ugly, Johnny thought as he watched it in the faint lamplight, but it had neither coldness nor hardness in it. It was as soft as a woman's face if you could manage to look past its ugliness. Now Doc turned his ponderous head and looked up.

"You two lift him carefully onto that door. Bring him to my house."

With Doc's help and that of the other man, Johnny got Arch Schilling's body onto the door. Then, Johnny and the other man lifted it and carried it out the door. Johnny heard Slade yelling something as he went out, but paid no attention to it.

It was obvious to him that Slade was scared. And if Slade was scared, it meant he didn't have a gun with which to defend himself. If he was still unarmed, then someone else had to have shot Arch. That someone could only be Ward Reeder or one of his two men.

Doc's house was three blocks from the jail. As they moved along the street, other men came from the shadows and helped to carry the door. By the time they reached Doc's place, seven men were carrying it.

Doc supervised them as they carried it inside. He had Arch placed on his big dining-room table. A couple of men carried out the door, on which there was a pool of blood.

Doc curtly directed his wife to light all the lamps she could find. He turned and looked at Johnny irritably, yet with compassion too. "Get out of here and do your job.

177

I'll do mine."

"Will he . . .? When . . .?"

"I'll send someone to tell you how he is when I get through with him. Now git!"

Johnny went out. He stood on the porch of Doc's house for several moments, long enough to roll and light a cigarette. If he hadn't gone out to Molly's for supper tonight . . .

He shook his head angrily. He couldn't have anticipated that Ward would be fool enough to shoot Arch. And Arch had told him to go. Even if he'd only gone to the hotel, it wouldn't have changed anything.

Slade! He'd been in town a single day and already one man was dead, another near to death, another facing a stiff term in prison if he was caught. And Slade sat it out in the jail, charged with nothing, free to leave town tomorrow if he chose.

The other men who had helped carry Arch stood in the darkness of Doc's lawn silently. There was a fragrance in the air — from blossoming lilacs somewhere nearby. One of the men said, "Is he . . .? Will Arch be all right?"

Johnny swung around irritably. "How the hell should I know? He's shot in the chest and damn few men . . ." He stopped suddenly. In a softer tone he said, "I'm sorry."

"Hell, forget it. We all know how you feel about Arch."

Johnny stepped down on the porch and walked away into the darkness. Behind him, he could hear them talking in lowered tones.

He felt like kicking something and he was scared. Scared that when Doc did send someone, it would be to tell him Arch was dead.

He reached Main. Lights glowed in the windows of both saloons and in the hotel. The rest of the street was dark.

He went into the Emporia and looked around. He didn't see Ward Reeder, or Willy or Les. He stopped just inside the door and yelled, "Did anybody see anything down at the jail just before you heard the shots?"

The buzz of talk quieted. There were a couple of men who seemed to be avoiding Johnny's eyes. Johnny crossed to them and said, "You two. What did you see?"

"It might not mean anything —"

"Damn you, what?"

"Well, we saw Les and Willy go in the jail before we heard the shots."

Johnny nodded. "Thanks." He turned and went back outside. Frowning, he walked toward the jail.

No one else would have reason for shooting Arch, he thought. No one else but Ward. If someone had tried breaking Slade out, Slade would have had a gun. Or he'd have been free. Only Ward Reeder would have panicked after shooting Arch. Only Ward would have panicked enough to run away.

He reached the jail and went inside. The two lamps were still burning on the table. From out back, Slade yelled. "That you, deputy?"

"Uh-huh." It occurred to Johnny that Slade must have been an eyewitness to Arch's shooting. He called, "You see the man that shot Arch?"

"Sure. It was Reeder. He was tryin' to get me."

A couple of men came in, carrying the door. The bloodstain had been wiped up but it still showed plainly. Johnny took the door from them, hung it and replaced the hinge pins in it. He closed it, leaving Slade in darkness. Slade was reasonably safe, he knew, as long as it was dark back there. The two men went away, subdued and silent.

Johnny sat down in the swivel chair and rolled a cigarette. He was alone now. Arch, even if he lived, would be laid up for weeks.

He thought of the four drifters again. He hadn't seen them in the crowd that had collected down here when they carried Arch out. He hadn't seen them in the Emporia or on the street. Not that their absence meant anything. Yet it bothered him, making a small stir of uneasiness in the back of his mind.

He finished his cigarette and threw the stub into the spittoon. He got up and paced uneasily back and forth. He kept thinking of Arch, how strong, how solid, how durable and tough the old man was. It seemed incredible to him that Arch now lay, pale and weak and unconscious, on Doc's dining-room table.

He walked back and opened the door leading to the cells. "I'm going out. I'll lock up. You'll be all right."

"With Reeder still loose? He can get in that window just as easy as he got out. He can shoot until he gets me."

Johnny said, "Right now I don't give a damn whether he does or not. I'm going to go see how Arch is getting along."

He slammed the door. He picked up the cell keys from the desk and put them in his pocket. He went out, locking the outside door behind him.

For a moment he stood there, his back to the door, feeling the cool night air stirring against his face. Even here, where the smells were of stable and saloon, the air still held a hint of lilac. The damn things must be blooming all over town.

The lilac made him think of Molly and thinking of her made him realize that nothing had been solved. Slade would still go free tomorrow. He would have to face Slade then, on the killer's own terms. He didn't see how that could be avoided.

He found himself wishing that Ward *would* get to Slade while he was gone. Maybe that was why he was leaving, he thought sourly. Maybe he was unconsciously or deliberately, giving Ward his chance.

He almost turned back. Then, shrugging, he walked quickly toward Doc's house.

The lamps were burning brightly in Doc's dining-room. Johnny walked around to the side of the house and stared in the window.

Arch's body was still stretched out on the table. Doc's wife was holding a lamp high while Doc bent over Arch's chest. There was blood on Doc's hands and on the instrument he held in one of them. As Johnny watched he turned and released the bullet to fall upon the floor.

He left the room, apparently to wash his hands because in a couple of minutes he returned, his hands now clean. He put a thick, folded compress on Arch's chest, then began to bandage him while his wife helped.

Johnny went around to the front of the house. He knocked, then went inside. "Can I help you move him to a bed?"

"I thought you'd gone."

"I came back. How is he, Doc? Is he going to make it all right?"

"He's got a chance. The bullet missed his lungs and heart. And he's pretty tough for a man his age."

"How soon . . ."

"Will I know?" Doc peered up at Johnny wearily. "A couple of hours will tell how he took the shock of getting the bullet out. If he gets over that all right, and if nothing unexpected comes up, then he'll probably live."

Johnny helped Doc Allen carry Arch to a bedroom and settle him in a bed. Leaving, he said, "I'll come back after a while."

"Yeah, Johnny. Do that. I'll stay with him until I'm sure he's going to make it through the night."

Johnny walked slowly toward the jail. Ward had probably ridden back out to his ranch, he thought, but he'd check until he had made sure.

Suddenly, in spite of himself, in spite of what Ward Reeder had done to Arch, he felt sorry for the man. Ward had lost his son and now had committed a felony. And the man who had killed Ward's son was still alive.

Chapter 16

Johnny walked back to Main and, quickly, along the near side of the jail. He crossed the street and unlocked the door. He lighted a lamp then walked to the rear door, opened it and called, "You all right?"

Slade only grunted sourly.

Johnny closed the door. Had his prisoner been anyone but Slade, he would probably have felt sorry for him. Slade was certainly a sitting duck, vulnerable to Ward's attempts to kill him, yet unable to defend himself.

He took time to roll a cigarette and light it. He frowned to himself. He hated to leave the jail again, to leave Slade unguarded, but he didn't see that he had much choice. Ward had shot Arch and if the sheriff died would have to stand trial for killing him. Furthermore, Ward Reeder was dangerous. He was desperate; he was tortured now by two things, guilt over the fact that he had shot Arch and the unavenged death of his son. There was no predicting what he might do next. The safest place for Ward was in jail. Only this time he'd go into one of the cells at the far rear of the jail, the ones that had no windows in them.

He blew out the lamp and went outside. He locked the door, then walked uptown toward the Emporia.

There was a crowd in the Emporia, but it was a shocked and subdued crowd. Johnny paused for a moment just inside the doors, looking the room over for Ward Reeder or either of his men. Then he crossed to the bar.

Sam drew a beer and brought it to him. Johnny asked, "Seen Ward, or Les, or Willy?"

"Not since Arch was shot. How is he, Johnny? Somebody said he'd been shot in the chest. Is he going to . . .?"

"Doc can't tell yet. He got the bullet out, but Arch lost a lot of blood. Doc won't know anything for a couple of hours. He said by then he'd know how Arch took the shock of getting the bullet out."

Sam nodded. Johnny gulped the beer. He saw the girl who had come in on the train with Slade talking to a couple of men at a corner table. "You hire her?"

Sam nodded.

"Think she knows Slade?"

Sam shrugged. "I didn't ask her that."

Johnny finished his beer and crossed the room. He said, "I see you got a job."

The girl smiled. The two with her, cowhands from a ranch twenty miles south of town, looked up at Johnny neutrally.

He pulled out a chair and straddled it, leaning his arms on the back. He watched the girl's face closely as he asked, "Do you know Slade Teplin?"

She shook her head, but did not meet his eyes and he knew that she had lied. He asked, "What's your name?"

She was a little paler now, and her eyes were scared. "Rose. Rose Malloy."

Johnny said, "I'm glad you don't know Slade. Knowing him could be dangerous."

She didn't reply. The two cowhands were staring at Johnny impatiently. He rose, nodded briefly and walked away. He went out and turned up the street toward the Ace-High. He stared into the darkness of the passageway between the two saloons as he passed it, but he saw nothing there.

He went into the Ace-High, stopping just inside the doors as he had at the Emporia. He turned and left when he failed to find Ward or either of his men.

He started toward the hotel, then stopped when a voice called out, "Johnny! Wait a minute. I want to talk to you."

He turned and waited. John McCracken had come out of the Ace-High and was now hurrying along the walk toward him.

McCracken stopped. "How's Arch?"

"He was shot in the chest. Doc got the bullet out and Arch is still alive. That's all I know for now."

"He should have let Ward kill the son-of-a bitch."

"You don't mean that. Ward would have gone to prison for it. That's what Arch was trying to prevent."

"Maybe I didn't mean that. I guess I didn't. But it seems to me there ought to be something . . . I mean it doesn't seem right that a killer like Slade can come here and wreck people's lives the way he has."

Johnny asked, "Have you seen Barney lately?"

McCracken shook his head.

Johnny said, "Why don't you go see him then? Along about now I'd bet he could use some shoring up. Are you going to fire him for getting drunk?"

McCracken hesitated, then said almost reluctantly, "I don't suppose so, as long as he doesn't get like he used to be."

"Then why not go tell him so?"

"Maybe I will. By God, maybe I will. It's a good idea." He turned and crossed the street. Halfway across he called back, "Thanks, Johnny."

Johnny turned in at the hotel. He crossed the whitetile lobby floor to the desk. Alf Holloway asked him about Arch, and Johnny gave him the same reply he'd given McCracken a few minutes before. Then he asked, "Which room has Ward Reeder got?"

"Seven. But he ain't —"

"Give me the key."

Alf shoved the key across the desk. Johnny took it and headed for the stairs.

In front of number seven he stopped. Carefully, he put his ear against the door panel. Then he knocked loudly.

He heard no sound inside — no sound at all. He inserted the key, turned it, then flung the door open with his left hand while with his right he drew his gun and thumbed the hammer back.

The room was dark. Johnny stepped inside, struck a match and looked around. The room was empty, but the bed was mussed as though someone had laid on it.

He went back out and re-locked the door. Down in the lobby, he returned the key to

189

Holloway. "If he comes in, you send someone to let me know. Understand?"

Alf nodded. Johnny crossed to the door and went outside again. He had looked all the obvious places for Ward. Alone, he couldn't comb the town. The best plan would be to wait for Ward down at the jail. Either Reeder had been so shocked after shooting Arch that he'd gone home to his ranch or else he'd try for Slade again.

He walked slowly along the street toward the jail. He couldn't help thinking of Molly and wondering how she was taking the suspense. He doubted if she'd stay out on Cottonwood Creek all night. She'd probably come in and stay with friends in town. Or take a room at the hotel.

On impulse, he whirled and returned to the hotel. He crossed the lobby to the desk. "I saw four strangers in town today. Drifters. Cowhands maybe. Did they take rooms here?"

Holloway shook his head. "I got no strangers registered."

Johnny nodded, turned and went back outside. He was frowning as he walked hurriedly toward the jail. There was a connection, he told himself, between Slade Teplin and the four strangers who had ridden in today.

There was a connection someplace if he could only figure out what it was.

He reached the jail, unlocked the door and went inside. He lighted a lamp and trimmed the wick. He opened the door leading to the cells.

The shot was almost deafening. A shower of splinters flew from the doorjamb beside Johnny's head. Half a dozen of them penetrated the skin of his face and one narrowly missed his eye. He flung himself back instantly, slamming the door as he did.

A second shot, muffled by the closed door, came closely on the heels of the first. This bullet tore a hole in the door-panel, chest high.

Ruefully, Johnny raised a hand and began to remove the splinters from his face. Slade Teplin had a gun. Or else Ward had returned and was now inside the cell he had formerly occupied.

Johnny yelled, "Slade?"

"Yeah. It's me, deputy. Who did you think it was?"

Someone had gotten a gun to him. The girl, Rose Malloy, knew him but she was with those two cowhands up at the Emporia. It had to have been one of the four drifters, Johnny thought. No one who lived in town would give Slade Teplin the time of day.

He stared uneasily into the darkness outside the office window. He resisted an impulse to go blow out the lamp. He suddenly wished that Arch was here. Because Slade Teplin was not alone in town. At least two of those drifters knew him and quite possibly all four of them did.

He ought to swear in some deputies, he thought. But he knew he'd have a hard time getting them.

In the first place, no one would serve as a deputy in order to protect Slade's life from Ward. Nor would their willingness to serve be increased by the knowledge that Slade had a gun.

But there was another cause for his reluctance, another reason even better than those two. He didn't want the town to think he couldn't handle the situation by himself. He didn't want anyone saying he was afraid of Slade.

And that was exactly what they would say if he asked for help. He had no proof the four drifters had any connection with Slade. He had no proof that Slade intended to break out of jail. Phil Regan might have slipped that gun to him simply because Phil was a troublemaker. Phil had egged Cal on earlier today. He wasn't above slipping a gun to Slade tonight.

He rolled a cigarette, sat down and put his feet up on the desk. He tried to relax his muscles but they remained tight-drawn and tense as a fiddlestring. If Ward came after Slade tonight, then Ward would get himself killed.

He got up and walked to the window. He began to pace nervously back and forth. On impulse, he blew out the lamp and opened the outside door.

Instantly a gun flared across the street. The glass beside Johnny shattered as the bullet struck.

He ducked back inside, slamming and locking the door. He stared across the street, trying to see the man who had shot at him.

Either the man was a damn poor shot or else he hadn't even tried to score a hit. Johnny was inclined to believe the latter theory.

They wanted him pinned down in here. They had him fixed so he could neither go outside nor go back to the cells where Slade was confined.

But why? What did they hope to accomplish? Until a few moments before, Slade had been confined only on a simple disturbance charge.

One thing seemed fairly sure. Slade wanted him dead but he wanted to do the killing himself. Else the man across the street would have killed him a minute or two before. There had been enough light in the street for that and he must have been silhouetted against the door.

It was a stand-off, then, for now. Johnny crossed the dark office and took a double-barreled ten gauge down from the rack. He loaded it, and took a handful of ten-gauge shells loaded with buckshot from a drawer of the desk.

He sat down on the office couch. The initiative belonged to Slade and all he could do was wait.

Slade's friends could do one of two things. They could get a team from the stable and yank the bars of Slade's cell out, the way Ward's two hired men had done. Or they could come through here, kill him and get the keys from him.

But why? For God's sake why? Slade would have been released tomorrow. Johnny scowled angrily in the darkness. He'd know what Slade's plan was before very long. If they didn't get him first.

Chapter 17

Molly stood at the kitchen doorway and watched Johnny ride away. She remained there, staring into the darkness long after he had gone, long after the sounds of his horse's hoofs had died away.

Turning, she began to pick up the dishes from the table. Her hands trembled violently and twice she almost dropped a stack of dishes. At last she gave up and sat down in one of the kitchen chairs. Tears filled her eyes and ran silently across her cheeks.

She had been wrong, she realized now. She should have divorced Slade long ago, when Johnny first asked her to marry him. Perhaps if she had . . .

Then she realized it would have changed nothing even if she had. Slade would still have returned eventually. He would have killed Johnny. Things would have been no different than they were right now.

Except for one thing. She would have been married to Johnny for a while. They would have had each other for that time, at least.

She got up hurriedly, washed the dishes and put them away. She got a light coat and put it on. She picked up a lantern, set it on the table and lighted it. She turned toward the door. She wasn't going to spend the night out here. She was going to town, where at least she would be near Johnny and know what was happening to him.

She heard a horse's hoofs approaching rapidly. She went to the door, expecting to see Johnny returning.

But it was not Johnny. It was a man she had never seen before. He dismounted in front of the kitchen door and asked, "Are you Molly Teplin, ma'am?"

"Yes. What is it?"

"I . . . I'm afraid I've got bad news for you."

Something cold, like an icy hand, closed around Molly's heart.

She forced herself to be calm. She asked, "What bad news? What's happened?"

"It's that deputy — Yoder, ma'am. He's been shot. The saloon-keeper asked me to ride out and tell you that."

"Shot . . .! How bad . . .?"

"I don't know, ma'am. I left right after it happened. Want me to help you hitch up your buggy horse?"

"Yes, please . . . if you would." She picked up the lantern, blew out the lamp and hurried out the door. She ran across the yard, the man striding along behind her, leading his horse.

She held the lantern while he led out the buggy horse and harnessed him. It seemed to take an eternity. The coldness inside her body had spread until she was cold all over. Johnny was dead, her mind kept telling her. It was over, because Johnny was dead. Slade had shot him and Slade never missed.

Numbly she climbed into the buggy. Numbly she handed the reins to the man, who had tied his saddle horse on behind. She said, "Hurry! Please hurry!"

He yelled at the buggy horse and slapped his back with the reins. The horse trotted away. The man kept yelling at him until he broke into a rocking lope.

Molly turned her head. "How did it happen? Who shot him?"

"I don't know who it was, ma'am. I didn't see it."

"Where did it happen?"

"In front of the saloon. I just rode up and the saloon-keeper yelled at me to ride out here. Maybe he's all right, ma'am. Maybe he ain't hurt bad at all."

Molly's lips formed the words of a prayer — that Johnny was alive — that he was not badly hurt. She cried, "Can't we go faster?"

"This horse, he won't go much faster, ma'am."

Shivering, Molly huddled in the corner of the buggy. She saw the town's lights, and heard the thunder of the horse's hoofs crossing the plank bridge. They rattled across the railroad tracks, then turned abruptly west. She screamed, "Where are we going? The saloons are on Main Stret!"

"You never mind, ma'am. I know what I'm doing."

She tried to wrest the reins from him but he shoved her back into the corner of the buggy. She tried to jump out, but he caught her arm in a powerful hand and held it. His fingers bit into her flesh cruelly.

For an instant she sat there frozen, overcome with a wild and sudden joy. He was not taking her to the saloon where he said Johnny had been shot. He was taking her someplace else, perhaps to Slade, and if part of his story was a lie, perhaps the rest of it was also a lie. Johnny might not have been shot at all.

Almost immediately, however, she was touched with fear. Wherever he was taking her, Slade would be waiting. And if Slade had ordered her brought to him it could only be for one reason. She was to be the bait in Slade's trap. Johnny was still alive, but she was to be the means by which Slade killed him.

The buggy drew to a halt in front of a small one-room shack. There was a rotting picket fence around the place and the yard was overgrown with weeds. No one had lived here for a couple of years, she knew. The house was deserted, its windows broken, its doors hanging open.

The man got out of the buggy without releasing her arm. He dragged her from the buggy after him. He said, "Come on, ma'am. Don't make no trouble now."

Molly opened her mouth to scream. The man's hand clamped over it, stifling the scream. She bit his hand savagely.

He yanked his hand away with an angry curse. He cuffed her on the side of the head, hard enough to make her senses reel. He dragged her into the house and kicked the door shut behind him.

She struggled violently, scratching, kicking, biting. He hit her again, this time with his fist.

She slumped, only half conscious, and he dragged her to a chair. He tied her to it with a coarse, rough-feeling lariat. He tied a bandanna around her mouth. By the time her senses had fully returned she was helpless, unable to cry out, unable to move.

The man rolled a cigarette and lighted it. He said, "Now we'll wait. We'll just relax and wait for Slade."

Occasionally, Johnny went to the window and stared across the street. His eyes were now accustomed to the darkness and he could make out the shadowy form of a man at the corner of a store building over there. He debated trying to shoot the man but gave up the idea because he knew he would be unable to see his sights.

He paced back and forth disgustedly. They certainly had him in a bind, he thought. He could go out, of course, and take a chance that the man would miss. But what could he do, even if he did get out? There were four of them.

No, he thought, his best chance lay in staying here, in forcing them to come to him. If they came in, he'd have a slight advantage over them. They'd be visible in the faint starlight in the street; he'd be hidden in the darkness here.

He heard voices from the cell block at the rear. A moment later he heard the sound of metal clanging against metal.

He charged toward the door and flung it open. He fired at the window of Slade's cell and heard the bullet ricochet and whine away into the night.

Instantly, a gun there in the cell opened up. A bullet clanged against one of the bars. A second buzzed past Johnny's ear like an angry bee.

He flung himself aside. He heard a man shout outside the jail and heard the rending sounds as the bars tore loose.

He poked his head around the doorjamb and fired again, ducking back to avoid the instant barrage that followed. He was glad this wall was brick. At least the bullets couldn't penetrate.

The air was now choked with powdersmoke. Bullets clanged regularly against the bars, or buzzed through the door, shattering the windows in the front of the office, thudding into the furniture, floor and walls.

And then, suddenly, all was quiet. Johnny

leaped through the door, gun in hand, hammer back.

The cells were empty. Slade Teplin was gone.

Johnny unlocked Slade's cell and went inside. He stared out the high window.

He could see the team standing there, their tugs still hitched to the chain that had been secured to the bars. But he saw nothing else.

Frowning, he returned to the office, went to the window and stared across the street. The shadowy figure was gone.

What in the hell did Slade have in mind, he wondered sourly. What was he up to now?

His immediate inclination was to leave the jail, round up some townsmen and arm them, then search the town for Slade. He did not understand his own reluctance to do so. Instead, he continued his pacing, scowling, trying to make sense out of this seemingly senseless jail break.

Slade hadn't had to get himself broken out of jail. He'd have been released in the morning anyway. It followed, therefore, that Slade had something he wanted to do tonight — something that wouldn't wait for tomorrow.

He crossed to the door and slowly, silently opened it. He retreated to the rear wall and stood there, the loaded ten gauge in his hands.

He didn't know how he knew, but he did. They would come to him. He was part of their plans, whatever those plans might be. Slade was crazy with hatred and the thirst for revenge. And Johnny was now number one on Slade's list because he was the one who had taken Slade's wife away from him.

The minutes dragged endlessly. Faintly, Johnny could hear the excited talk uptown. They had heard the shots, he realized. But they wouldn't help. They'd figure this was his job. None of the townsmen were fighting men. They just simply didn't know what to do.

And it was his job. Now that Arch had been shot, it was Johnny's job.

He wondered how Arch was. Doc ought to know by now whether Arch was going to make it or not. He wished he could leave and go to Doc's house. He wished he could find out.

He heard a scuffing sound outside at the corner of the jail. He held his breath for a moment and froze exactly where he was. He stared through the shattered windows into the starlit street.

"Deputy." It was a voice he had never heard before, calling softly from the corner of the building outside. He did not reply.

"Hey, deputy. I got something to tell you."

Still Johnny did not reply. His breathing was slow, quiet, controlled, but his hands were shaking as they gripped the shotgun stock.

He saw the man's head as he peered into the window. He saw the man's form cautiously emerge from concealment and approach the door.

He laid the shotgun down carefully on the floor. The man would be coming in through the door in another minute. He could shoot him, but he wanted him alive. He wanted to know exactly what Slade was planning now.

The man came through the door. He had a gun in his hand and he tried to peer into the corners of the room, tried to pierce the darkness with his glance. He came as far as the center of the room and whispered, "Deputy? You here?"

Johnny's muscles were tense. He was crouched, silent, ready. The man turned back toward the door.

And Johnny launched himself. He plunged across the room like a great, silent beast of prey.

Chapter 18

At the first sound from behind, the man whirled. Before he could line his gun, before he could fire, Johnny struck him with the point of his shoulder in the chest.

He was flung back helplessly. He crashed into the unbroken window on the left side of the door, shattering it.

Johnny was on him like a wolf, grappling for his throat. The man rolled among the broken shards of glass from the window, and brought up a savage knee that caught Johnny in the groin.

Johnny's hands closed around his throat. Both hands and throat were bloody from glass cuts and it was like trying to clutch a greased pig. The man thrashed violently. Johnny released his throat and smashed his fist into the stranger's face.

He straddled the man, trying to ignore the fiery pain in his groin and lower abdomen.

His fists smashed methodically into the man's face.

The man still held his gun. He rammed it against Johnny's side.

Johnny groped for it frantically. His hand closed over the cylinder just as the hammer fell.

It fell on the loose skin between his thumb and forefinger, cutting through, causing such a sharp pain that Johnny grunted involuntarily. But the gun did not fire. Johnny wrenched it away and batted the man on the side of the head with it.

It struck only a glancing blow. The man arched his body convulsively, flinging Johnny off and to one side. He scrambled to his feet and staggered toward the door.

Johnny plunged after him, the gun still hanging from his hand. He caught the man's ankles in a flying dive and brought him crashing down, inches short of the door. The man brought both legs up close to him and kicked out violently with both feet.

One foot caught Johnny squarely in the face. The heel took him on the chin, the sole squarely on the nose. He could feel the warmth of blood spurting from it.

The kick stunned him briefly, but he groped until he had regained his grip. The man sat up and began to flail Johnny with his fists. Johnny released his ankles and swung wildly with the hand in which the gun still hung.

He missed and the gunhammer tore through the flesh of his hand. The gun skidded across the room. The man turned and scrambled after it.

Johnny plunged after him. He landed on the man's back while his hand was still inches short of the gun. He seized the man's hair and began to slam his head methodically against the glass-strewn floor. But his hands were so bloody and slick that he lost his grip.

He fought with a single-minded concentration that excluded all else from his consciousness. He had been all but helpless since Slade Teplin had come in on the train. Now his frustration was coming out. He was hurt and bloody and had little to gain from this. But he was enjoying it as he had enjoyed nothing since he had jumped Slade earlier in the Emporia. He was revenging Arch, who would not have been shot had it not been for Slade. He was revenging Molly for the anguish she had felt all day. And he was revenging himself.

The stranger broke away, got up and

plunged toward the door once more. Johnny, charging across the room after him like a maddened bull, struck him and bowled him bodily aside, into the desk, over its top, to fall on the opposite side in the wreckage of the kerosene lamp that had been sitting on the desk.

Johnny followed him over the desk-top and landed once more on top of him. The man was fighting with a silent desperation now, fighting for his life. Each blow he struck had a sodden, smacking sound because both his fists and Johnny's face were wet with blood. And he was tough. He was wiry and strong and no stranger to this kind of fight.

But he lacked one thing, one thing that Johnny had – anger, righteous indignation and outraged fury. Johnny had these things in quantity. For every blow the stranger struck, Johnny retaliated with another, harder one.

The man was weakening. They rolled across the glass-strewn floor to the window and back again. And at last Johnny felt the man go limp.

He stumbled to his feet and for a long, long time stood there, head hanging, lungs working like a gigantic bellows. His belly still hurt from the kick he had received early in the fight. His nose still bled. His hands were two masses of glass cuts and the pain from the mangled flesh, torn by the gunhammer, was excruciating still.

He glanced toward the door uneasily. It didn't seem logical that the man had come alone but Johnny was relieved that no one else appeared. He was in no condition to fight anyone else right now.

When he could breathe again with some normality, he stopped and grasped the man beneath his shoulders. He dragged him through the door into the cell corridor. He dragged him into one of the cells at the far rear, those with no windows in them.

Weakly, nearly exhausted by the exertion, he sat down on the bunk. He still didn't know what the man had come here to tell him. What he did know was that he had cut down the odds. Instead of being five to one, they were now only four to one.

On the stone floor, the man stirred, and groaned. Johnny stared at him apathetically. It was almost completely dark in here, but there was enough light to see the man's dark-lumped shape lying on the floor. The man groaned again.

Johnny said softly, "You're going to talk,

you son-of-a-bitch, or I'm going to kick your head in. You understand what I said?"

The man raised his head groggily. On hands and knees he tried to scramble out the open cell door into the corridor.

Johnny got up, circled him and took a position in front of the door. The man stopped crawling. Johnny said, "You got just one more chance."

The man tried to get up. Johnny kicked him deliberately. He had no real stomach for what he was doing, but he had to know what was in the air. Four drifters and Slade. They added up to real trouble for the town. They added up to more than Slade's personal revenge against two or three individuals.

The man laid still for a long, long time. Johnny said softly, "You may not be able to talk by the time I get through with you. But you'll be able to write if you have to write on the floor with your own damn blood."

The man made it to his hands and knees. Johnny moved to one side and kicked him in the stomach. The man collapsed again.

Twice more the man got to his hands and knees. Twice more Johnny kicked him down. At last the man groaned softly, "All right. All right. To hell with Slade anyway."

"What's going on? What's he planning to do?"

"He's got his wife in a shack down on the edge of town. He told me to tell you the old Montoya place. He figured you'd come down there and he could kill you in front of her."

Johnny felt his fury growing. Slade had Molly. If he'd hurt her . . .

He said harshly, "What else?"

"That's all."

Johnny drew back his foot angrily. The man yelled, "Wait!"

"All right, you son-of-a-bitch! What else?"

"It's the bank. They're going to clean it out, and burn what's left, papers, records and everything. He wants more than the money. He wants to break the town."

Johnny crossed the cell and went out into the corridor. He closed the cell door, locked it and dropped the keys into his pocket. He felt automatically for his gun but his hand encountered only an empty holster.

He returned to the shambles the fight had made of the office and searched around until he found his gun. Crossing the room, he picked up the loaded ten gauge from the floor.

He went to the door and peered outside. There was still a knot of men up in front of the two saloons, but it had thinned out some. Johnny knew he ought to go up there. He ought to alert the townsmen to the danger. They could scatter, arm themselves and be back in ten minutes at the most.

Hesitating, he stood in front of the jail, wiping his bleeding hands on the sides of his pants. He thought of Molly, with Slade. It would please Slade to assert his rights as Molly's husband. Even if he had to do it on the dirty floor of a deserted shack.

He couldn't afford ten minutes. He couldn't afford any time at all. To hell with the bank. Molly was more important now.

Turning, he hurried along the street toward the lower end of town.

The shotgun was slick with blood in his hand. Twice, he shifted it to the other hand and wiped the one it had been in on his trouser leg. Three strangers and Slade. He wondered how many of the strangers were there with Slade.

How had they gotten Molly to town, to the old Montoya place? Probably by telling her he'd been hurt, he thought. Damn them. Damn them!

He turned the corner just short of the railroad station. He followed the tracks for half a block, then turned right again. The old Montoya house loomed up in the darkness ahead.

A soft breeze blew toward him from the creek. He could hear the sound of the water, and the rustling of the cottonwoods.

He stopped and stared at the dilapidated house. He could make out nothing, no shadows, no movements that might have been made by men. There was only one way to do this, he decided. Let them know that he was here. Force them to take the initiative.

He raised the shotgun and let go one barrel at the house. The roar of the gun was deep and sonorous, echoing and re-echoing through the town. The shot rattled against the walls and roof.

Temporarily blinded by the flash, Johnny flung himself to the ground. In the window of the Montoya place a revolver flashed, then again and again. Johnny got up and sprinted up the street, beyond the house, to fall prone again.

The revolver barked twice as he sprinted past the house. He could hear the bullets tearing into the building wall behind him.

But he had learned one thing. He knew with reasonable certainty that only one man was in the house. By staying here an instant more he would find out if any others were waiting for him outside the house.

He held his breathing quiet and reloaded the empty shotgun barrel. The gun made a click as he snapped the action shut.

He crouched there, searching the shadows with his glance. Then, suddenly, he got up and ran directly across the street, weaving and zig-zagging as he ran.

Again the revolver barked. Johnny felt a sharp pain in his right shoulder and realized he had been hit. He flung himself over the sagging fence and rolled to a halt in the high, thick weeds, only a dozen yards from the door.

He heard Slade Teplin yell, "Molly! He's out here! Yell out and tell him who you want to be married to!"

Johnny called softly, "I've got a ten gauge, Slade. Two barrels loaded with buck. And I'm close enough to cut you in two."

There was no answer from the house. Johnny called, "I'm going to stand up, I'm coming in. You shoot, Slade, and I'll have a target to put this buckshot in."

"Molly's here!"

"Is she? All I've got is your word for that."

"Damn you, woman, sing out!"

Johnny heard a cry of pain. Molly was there all right. He would have known her voice anywhere. He froze where he was, knowing he didn't dare spray that flimsy house with buckshot now.

He called, "I'm going to the bank, Slade. Your man spilled everything he knew. If you want to kill me, you'll have to come up there."

He began to crawl forward through the weeds. Slade emptied his gun again, yelling as he did, "God damn you, deputy, if you go now you'll find Molly dead when you come back!"

Johnny crawled until he reached the corner of the house. He leaped to his feet and ran to a side window.

He had only the briefest glance as he rammed the shotgun through the window, the briefest kind of glance into a pitch-dark room. He saw three squares of light and nothing else. Two windows and a door. He could make them out because of the starlight beyond in the street.

He didn't see Molly; he didn't see anything in the room. But then he saw a

216

shadow silhouetted dimly against the door, a shadow that could only be Slade.

Slade was diving frantically, falling even as Johnny fired the left barrel of the gun. The roar, the flash, filled the room with sound and light. In this light he saw Molly, bound to a chair, and he saw Slade rolling on the ground outside.

He scrambled through the window frantically. At least, he thought fleetingly, he had separated Slade from Molly. He had put himself between the two.

He tripped and fell as he plunged across the room toward the door. He recovered and plunged on. At the doorway he stopped, raised the gun and fired at the dimly seen, running shape.

Slade, halfway across the street, staggered and nearly fell. Then he disappeared behind the building across the street.

Johnny reloaded the gun. He turned, fumbling for his pocket knife. He whispered, "Molly, are you hurt?"

"No. I'm . . ." She was trembling violently and close to hysteria.

Johnny said, "I'm all right, too. Now listen. Will you do what I tell you to?"

"Johnny, please . . ."

His voice turned sharp. "Molly! Listen!

It's important that you do exactly what I tell you to."

He finished cutting her loose. Careful not to touch her with his bloody hands, he kissed her lightly on the cheek. She whispered, "I'll do whatever you say, Johnny."

"Good. Leave here by the back door. Head for the creek. When you reach it, follow it south and stay out of sight. At the footbridge, leave it and head for the school. Wait for me there."

"All right." Her voice still trembled on the brink of hysteria. "Be careful, Johnny. Please."

"I will. Now hurry."

He heard the floorboards creak as she left the room, went through the kitchen and out onto the back porch. He heard the rustling of the weeds out back. Then, with a soft sigh of relief, he headed for the door. He'd hit Slade a moment or so before. He'd hit him hard enough to make him stagger and nearly fall. Maybe he'd find him over by that building wall.

He crossed the street cautiously. He reached the building across the street and moved carefully to the corner of it where Slade had disappeared. But Slade was gone.

He headed toward the bank, staying in the

alley, walking carefully. He still had four of them to face, but it was better than five. At least Molly was safe. He was in a better position than before. Even if there wasn't much chance that he would win.

Chapter 19

To Slade Teplin, there was nothing quite so terrifying as a shotgun. He had seen what a shotgun could do to a man. He had seen men with their heads literally blown off by a shotgun charge.

He ran along the building wall through the high-grown weeds, limping from a pellet that had penetrated his leg. He cursed softly, savagely to himself.

Nothing had gone right for him since he'd arrived on the train this morning. Almost everything had gone wrong. This town was a goddamn jinx. Or so it seemed. Yet he had to concede that it hadn't all been bad. He'd gotten Barney drunk, and that had been part of his plan. Before he left town tonight he'd loot and burn the bank. The only thing he had failed to do was get that deputy and he'd still have another chance at him.

He turned up the alley toward the bank. He knew this town as well as any of its inhabitants. He'd grown up here.

Russ and Joe had gone after Barney. Del was supposed to be waiting at the back door of the bank. The fourth man, Brothers, had gone to the jail to bring Yoder to the old Montoya house. He didn't know where Brothers was now. Yoder might have killed him — or thrown him in jail.

Del was waiting for him at the back door of the bank. Slade whispered, "How's the street out front? Any people there?"

"What's the matter with you? You're limping."

"Shotgun pellet. Don't worry about it."

"The street's pretty near deserted now. A lot of men came out of the saloons when the ruckus started at the jail and later when you and Yoder shot it out. They've gone back in."

"All right, come on. Russ and Joe ought to be along with Barney pretty soon."

He had told them to bring Barney even if they had to carry him. He wanted more than Barney's keys. He wanted Barney himself. He wanted to leave his father in the bank so the whole town would know how he'd gotten in. Let Barney live that down. Let him try living in a town whose inhabitants blamed him for ruining them.

He walked silently along the passageway between the bank and the building next to it. He reached the street and peered out carefully.

He saw Russ and Joe coming down the street from the direction of Barney's house, supporting him between them. He was drunk, all right, but he was not passed out.

They reached the passageway. Barney's head lolled drunkenly. He said thickly, "So itsh you! I mighta knowed!"

Slade said, "Shut up."

Russ said, "The banker was there with him. Joe rapped him on the head."

"You got Barney's keys?"

"Yeah." Russ handed the keys to him. Slade said, "Wait here out of sight. If he tries to yell, stuff something in his mouth."

He glanced up and down the street. Seeing no one, he went to the door of the bank, inserted the key and opened it. He beckoned and the others came in, dragging Barney along.

Slade said, "You got all the horses?"

"They're tied a couple of doors up the street. In front of the Emporia so they wouldn't draw attention."

"Then let's get busy. Russ, you stay here at the door."

Del and Joe dragged Barney through the waist-high gate and back toward the safe at the rear of the bank, following Slade. Slade knelt in front of it and struck a match.

"You know the combination?" Del asked.

Slade said contemptuously. "Don't have to. They never spin the knob. They turn it right to ten and all I have to do is turn it back until it clicks."

He turned the knob slowly, carefully. He stopped, and swung the safe door open. He glanced around and up. "Got the kerosene?'

"It's outside in that little passageway."

"Get it."

Del left. Slade began to remove canvas money sacks from the safe. He placed them in a small pile beside him on the floor. Then he began to rake papers out. They made a good-sized pile next to the money sacks. Notes, abstracts, mortgages. He laid the bank's record books on top of the pile. Then he gathered up the money sacks.

Barney was mumbling drunkenly, but his words were not understandable. Slade said, "Drag him up front and hit him with your fist. I want him here, but I don't want him to burn to death."

Joe began to drag Barney toward the front of the bank. Slade picked up the money sacks and carried them after him. He handed them to Russ, waiting at the door. Joe's fist, hitting Barney's jaw, made a sharp crack. Barney slumped and Joe laid him down at one side of the door.

Del came back with a can of kerosene. Slade took it from him and carried it back to the safe. He poured it over the bank's books and papers. He reached in his pocket for a match.

Slade struck the match and flung it on the pile. It caught immediately, blazing up halfway to the ceiling. Drawing his gun he ran for the front door.

A gun began to bark steadily in the street. Del staggered out the door and fell on the boardwalk. Joe was driven back and also fell, twisting and writhing with agony on the floor. Russ, down below window level, shouted furiously, "That fire! It made targets out of us and we can't see a goddamn thing!"

He got up and sprinted out the door, carrying the money sacks. He didn't get ten steps. He doubled, ran another two steps that way, then fell on his face and laid still, the money sacks scattered in front of him.

Slade stared for an instant in unbelief. Only one gun was firing out there and it had momentarily stopped, probably while the shooter reloaded it.

He turned and ran for the rear door of the bank, raging inwardly. He hadn't realized the fire would make targets of everyone inside the bank. God damn this town to hell! God damn that deputy . . . !

The rear door had a padlock on it. Slade fired and the lock sprung open. He snatched it out of the hasp and flung open the door. He plunged blindly into the dark alley and began to run.

When Johnny Yoder reached the rear door of the bank. Slade and his two companions had already gone. Johnny halted for a moment, hesitating. Then he returned the way he had come until he reached another passageway. He ran along it to the street, avoiding tin cans and debris.

He reached the street and without slackening his pace, turned left and headed toward the bank, angling out into the street as he did. On the far side of the street, directly across from the bank, he stopped.

This range was too great for the shotgun, he judged, and laid it aside. He drew his revolver, checked the loads absently, then thumbed the hammer back. If they went out the back door, he would lose them. But he could see that the front door of the bank was open, and he suspected that their horses were among those tied in front of the Emporia. They'd probably come out this way.

He saw a shadow leave the door and enter the passageway. A moment later, the shadow returned and disappeared into the open door of the bank.

The waiting seemed endless. Johnny realized he was foolish for trying to handle this all by himself. But he also knew there wasn't time to alert anyone else now. He had no choice but to handle it himself.

If only it wasn't so dark! If he could only see better, so that when the time for it came, he could shoot.

He waited, his hands shaking noticeably. It was quiet, over there. The only sounds in the street were the muffled sounds of voices in the two saloons. He hoped nothing would bring men crowding out into the street. He didn't want any bystander casualties if it could be helped.

Suddenly the whole front window of the bank lighted up. Johnny could see flame in the rear of the bank, leaping high, nearly to the ceiling. And he could see the men . . . three of them.

He fired instantly. One of the men staggered out the door and crumpled on the walk. Another was driven back into the bank. He also fell and Johnny lost sight of him.

He held his fire momentarily, punching out empties, punching in fresh shells. He saw Slade run toward the front of the bank. He drew a bead but did not squeeze the trigger because Slade ducked down out of sight.

Suddenly another man leaped to his feet and plunged out the door. This one was loaded with canvas money sacks. Johnny followed him with his gun, the sights showing plainly against the reddish light caused by the fire. He fired.

The man seemed to stumble. Crouched, he ran a couple of more steps before he fell. Switching his glance back to the bank door, Johnny saw Slade running toward the rear. Before he could get his sights on the man, Slade disappeared.

Johnny snatched up the shotgun, ramming the revolver into its holster as he did. He sprinted across the street.

Men were pouring out of the two saloons. Johnny bawled, "The bank! There's a fire in there! Get after it!"

He plunged into the passageway next to the bank, and ran along it recklessly. He reached the alley and skidded to a halt, swinging the shotgun toward the rear door of the bank.

It was open. Slade was gone. He hesitated a moment, glancing up and down the alley. It was almost completely dark, except for the small amount of light shed by the stars. Holding himself completely still, Johnny listened. From his left he heard the scuffing sounds of a man's running feet.

Instantly he turned and plunged after them. He was out of breath, both from running and from excitement, but he realized that he would never have a better chance at Slade than he had right now. Three of Slade's companions were either wounded or dead. Another was in jail. Slade was all alone and furthermore, his chance of forcing Johnny into a duel of speed and accuracy was gone. This was a hunt and while Slade was armed and dangerous, his greatest advantage was gone.

Slade reached the street, briefly visible. Then he plunged out of sight to the right.

Johnny followed recklessly, well aware that Slade was probably waiting for him, waiting to fire until he would run out of the alley into the open.

He reached the street and raced out into it, not turning until he reached the middle.

Swinging around, he saw that Slade had stopped. Slade was waiting beside a high board fence, facing Johnny, his gun in his hand.

In that split second, Johnny saw something else. He saw three more men up at the corner of Main and knew instantly who they were. Ward Reeder, and Les and Willy, his hired men.

He flung himself aside, falling, trying to bring the shotgun to bear. Slade's gun spat wickedly and the bullet grazed his thigh, burning like a hot iron.

The light was bad for shooting, but Johnny didn't need light if he could only bring the shotgun to bear before Slade could shoot again. Rolling, he swung it around and thumbed one hammer back.

Up at the corner, three more guns opened up, laying a concentrated fire against the fence. Johnny could hear the bullets tearing through the boards.

Slade hesitated between shooting at Johnny

and defending himself against the other three. He hesitated for the smallest part of a second but it was enough. Johnny squeezed the shotgun's trigger and felt it buck against his hands.

Shot rattled against the fence like hail. Slade's gun fired, but it was pointed at the sky. Johnny got up and ran toward him, thumbing the second hammer back. He heard the sounds of other running feet.

He reached Slade, who was motionless on the ground. He stirred Slade with his boot.

Ward and his two men charged up. Johnny swung the shotgun. "Easy, damn you. Drop those guns or I'll cut you in two."

The guns thudded to the ground. Johnny said, "Ward, you and Les pick him up. Take him down in front of the bank."

Meekly, Reeder picked up Slade's head and shoulders. Les picked up his feet. Willy supported his sagging body in the middle. They shuffled silently toward Main, turned the corner and headed for the bank.

Johnny felt weak. He felt as though he might be going to fall. He gritted his teeth and shook his head savagely against the mounting dizziness in it.

Men were coming toward him. Down in

front of the bank there were forty or fifty men, forming a bucket brigade, running in and out of the bank. Slade's companions had been dragged out of the way and now lay in a neat row, side by side. On the chest of the middle one were piled the canvas money sacks.

Followed by half a dozen men, Johnny herded his prisoners to the bank. He said, "Lay him down. Ward, you see if he's dead."

They laid Slade down and Ward picked up his wrist. He turned and looked up at Johnny. "He's dead. The son-of-a-bitch is dead."

"All right. Head for the jail."

He followed them down the street to the jail. He herded them in, watched while they threaded through the office wreckage and meekly entered the other cell at the far rear. He fumbled in his pocket until he found the key. He locked the door.

Only now did he break the shotgun and take the live shell out. He returned to the office, closing the door behind him.

A crowd of more than a dozen men were waiting in front of the jail. Johnny went out, leaving the shotgun behind. The wounds in his thigh and shoulder had begun to burn fiercely.

He said, "A couple of you stay here and watch this place. Get hold of Ern Powers and have him come down and clean things up."

Limping slightly, he turned and walked slowly toward the bank. He was thinking of Molly, thinking that nothing now stood in their way. He was heading toward the school when he suddenly saw her pass the bank, holding up her skirt so that she wouldn't trip, running like a frightened deer.

She reached him and flung herself into his arms, sobbing hysterically. "You're hurt!"

"Nothing serious." He held her close, feeling her trembling, feeling her softness and her warmth. He bent his head and kissed her, and felt the wetness of tears on her soft, smooth cheek.

The specter of death, which had hovered all day over Cottonwood Springs, was gone. Tomorrow it would be the same sleepy, pleasant town it had been yesterday. Johnny said, "Let's walk over to Doc's and see how Arch is getting along."

Limping, with Molly supporting him, he crossed the street and headed for Doc

Allen's house. He was thinking that they weren't going to wait any longer. They were going to get married tomorrow. The waiting was at an end.

THORNDIKE PRESS HOPES you have enjoyed this Large Print book. All our Large Print titles are designed for the easiest reading, and all our books are made to last. Other Thorndike Press Large Print books are available at your library, through selected bookstores, or directly from the publisher. For more information about our current and upcoming Large Print titles, please send your name and address to:

THORNDIKE PRESS
ONE MILE ROAD
P.O. Box 157
THORNDIKE, MAINE 04986

There is no obligation, of course.